WIRED TARGET

Paradise Crime Thrillers Book 14

TOBY NEAL

NOTE TO READERS:

"Our revenge will be the laughter of our children."
~ Bobby Sands

Important note for those following both series:
Sophie's Paradise Crime Thrillers take place in the five-year gap between Rip Tides #9 and Bone Hook #10 in the Lei's Paradise Crime Mystery timeline.

Copyright Notice

This is a work of fiction. Names, characters, businesses, places, events, and incidents are either the products of the author's imagination or used in a fictitious manner. Any resemblance to actual persons, living or dead, or actual events is purely coincidental.

© Toby Neal 2022

http://tobyneal.net/

ISBN: 979-8-9857068-3-3

ALL RIGHTS RESERVED. This book contains material protected under International and Federal Copyright Laws and Treaties. Any unauthorized reprint or use of this material is prohibited. No part of this book may be reproduced or transmitted in any form or by any means, electronic or mechanical, including photocopying, recording, or by any information storage and retrieval system, without express written permission from the author/publisher.

Cover Design: Jun Ares

Format Design: Neal Enterprises, INC.

❦ Created with Vellum

1

Day 1

Back to work after six months of maternity leave, investigator Sophie Smithson tightened her hold on the sissy strap of a heavy-duty Ford truck as it bumped through a red dirt pothole on the way to Oahu's scenic bird sanctuary at Ka'ena Point. Marcus Kamuela, a detective with Honolulu Police Department, gripped the wheel tightly as they hit another chuckhole. "Good thing I was able to get this permit for us to drive out to the sanctuary, or we would have had to walk all the way to the crime scene."

Sophie glanced at Kamuela. The detective's jaw was tight, his brown eyes intent behind mirrored sunglasses as he navigated the rough road through the state park toward the windswept, most northwestern point on the island. "This was one of my favorite run-hike routes before the babies were born."

"Ka'ena Point's popular, even though it's a two and a half mile hike each way, with no shade, water, or facilities."

"I enjoy this trail," Sophie said. "I've been hoping to do it again. But given that we're on the clock, driving is more efficient."

Wedged behind Sophie sat her colleague Pierre Raveaux, his knees folded high in the truck's narrow passenger seat. "Going out to the scene in person is always a good starting point on a case," he said. "*Merci beaucoup* for making the time to show us the area."

"The client waited for me to come back to work before moving ahead with contracting Security Solutions," Sophie said. "We appreciate you being willing to work with us."

"Honolulu Police Department's glad for the help at this point because we haven't had time to give this case the man-hours it needs, even though public outrage has created pressure. As you know, I work in the Homicide Division, and this was a crime involving animals . . . or birds, I should say." Beads of sweat had formed on Kamuela's broad brow despite the truck's air-conditioning, and he swiped a beefy, tattooed forearm across his forehead. "Nobody can understand why someone would sneak into a nature preserve and kill twelve adult Laysan albatrosses and smash their eggs."

"I understand the press are calling it the Moli Massacre," Raveaux said. "*Moli* being the Hawaiian name for the Laysan albatross."

"Yes, and that's why HPD put me on the case rather than letting the Department of Land and Natural Resources be the only agency to investigate. According to the experts I interviewed, damage to future generations of this endangered species is hard to calculate exactly, but huge," Kamuela said.

Sophie shut her eyes, trying not to imagine the scene that had met the sight of park staffers the morning after the savage attack on the peaceful birds at their nesting grounds had taken place. "This is cowardly of me, but I'm glad there won't be much to see three months later."

"The park rangers cleaned up the mess." Kamuela's jaw was tight. "The photos will be grisly enough for you to review. I've seen some dark things in my time, but this was one of the worst. Give me a crime involving humans any day."

Sophie gazed out the window at the passing scenery to distract herself. Kaʻena Point was a dry area of the island; no large trees broke up the rolling sand dunes, sparkling turquoise ocean, and scrubby bushes that dotted the arid landscape.

On the left, towering cliffs in bold red volcanic soil studded with boulders and a few wind-battered *haole koa* and *kiawe* trees set off the ocean's fringe of yellow-white coral beach and aquamarine surf over barrier reefs.

Gruesome case aside, it was exciting to be back in the field after the last three months spent exclusively in the company of her boyfriend Connor, nanny Armita, toddler Momi, and infant Sean. Armita, Momi and Sean awaited Sophie at her home in Kailua, but she'd had to say a wrenching goodbye to Connor when she left his private island of Phi Ni in Thailand.

Even now, the ocean she gazed at reminded her of his sea-colored eyes . . .

"I'm assuming you will let us review the surveillance video, too," Raveaux said from behind Sophie. "I did a quick scan of your case file, which mentions that two male perpetrators were visible in the footage."

"You're welcome to review it further, but the perps knew the park's cameras were recording and where they were located. The killers wore bandannas over their faces as well as ball caps on their heads. Other than being able to ascertain that there were two males, both less than six feet tall, one skinny, one heavy, there isn't much to go on. We couldn't even make out skin tone in the low-quality feed."

"Those details show premeditation, though," Sophie said. "The Moli Massacre was not an impulse crime."

Kamuela glanced at her; Sophie was struck as she'd been in the past by the man's handsome Hawaiian features, and how fierce he looked when he frowned. "I can't promise that I'd be able to follow due process if I got my hands on the perps. In our culture, the *moli* are some of our most revered `*aumakua*, guardian spirits of the ancestors. We treat these birds with utmost respect." He blew out a breath. "Albatrosses are large but have little fear of humans. From what we could tell from the scene, they did not defend themselves."

Sophie looked out the window again. Even murders she'd worked didn't get to her like the slaughter of these rare birds; apparently Kamuela felt the same.

The detective and investigators reached a red dirt parking area at the end of the road. A tall chain-link fence with a turnstile gate and an information kiosk marked the entrance to the sanctuary.

Kamuela parked the truck, pointing to the high barrier. "Private citizens raised funds to fence this entire section of the park to protect the *moli's* nesting grounds. That fence keeps out mongooses, pigs, and feral cats, which would disturb the birds and feed on their eggs. Unfortunately for the birds, it's designed to allow humans to pass through."

Sophie got out of the cab of the truck, flipping the seat lever so that Raveaux could climb out as well. Raveaux dusted down his trousers as he straightened up from the cramped quarters. He wore a battered but quality pale straw fedora and a pair of Ray-Ban aviators with a white linen shirt; Raveaux was always a notch better dressed than anyone else. Their mutual friend, forensic auditor Hermoine Leede, called Raveaux's elegance "the Paris factor."

The three donned backpacks containing water and their crime kits. Kamuela held aloft a large plastic bag. "Might as well pick up some trash while we're at it."

They proceeded through the turnstile and walked along a well-worn path between sturdy native bushes and clumps of grass. A boulder-strewn beach they navigated was empty and stunning; gentle waves lapped against golden sand studded with white coral.

Brisk wind tugged at Sophie's curly hair, still thick and long from pregnancy. She swung her arms as she walked, enjoying the strength she was rebuilding; the physical effects of carrying, birthing, and feeding a baby were no small feat for any woman, even the fittest.

Kamuela interrupted Sophie's rumination with a touch on her shoulder. "Look."

The three of them paused, gazing at a meter-high albatross standing majestically on its nest, a large, speckled white egg balanced between sturdy yellow webbed feet.

The *moli* stood tall, its snowy feathers reflecting the sunshine. The bird's far-seeing eyes, framed by sooty black feathers like Egyptian eyeliner, gazed at the three humans with neither fear nor aggression. The nest was a simple construction of twigs and feathers; the egg itself was at least the size of a mango.

Marcus spoke softly as they walked past. "Volunteers from the local Audubon Society as well as our park service personnel cleaned up the remains after the attack. I just want to check and see if we missed anything."

He described the scene as he and the other staffers had seen it right after the massacre. "You can view the photos back at the station when you look at our case file in more detail, but the perps came armed with weapons. As you said, Sophie, the attack was premeditated."

They passed a few more of the giant birds, grooming each other and sunning themselves. At no time did any of them show fear or aggression toward the humans passing through their domain.

Sophie had already been predisposed to not only taking the case but taking it seriously; now that she had seen the regal birds in their native habitat, the deep burn of outrage under her sternum would provide fuel for the investigation in the days to come.

The trio did a thorough walk-through of the birds' nesting area. Sophie took reference photos of the cameras positioned near the entrance and exit of the fenced protective zone. "Did you ascertain whether the perps came in by vehicle?" Sophie asked. "That might provide a source of clues."

"They did not come in by car that we can tell," Marcus said. "No permits for vehicle usage were issued the day of the attack, and the gate to the road we used was locked."

"That's a long hike at night, and a good distance back in the dark after the deed was accomplished," Raveaux said as they exited the nesting area. "Maybe the killers camped somewhere close."

"Camping isn't permitted anywhere in the park, but you're right. That's a possibility. We searched extensively inside the protected zone, but not much along the trail," Kamuela said as they approached his truck.

Raveaux raised his brows at Sophie. "What do you think? Should we hike back and look for a campsite?"

"Sounds good to me, as long as we can get some more water from you, Marcus," Sophie said.

Kamuela popped open the side door of the vehicle to expose a flat of water bottles. "I'll do you one better and loan you a hat." He clapped an HPD ball cap on Sophie's head. "Unfortunately, I can't come with you—got a fresh homicide back at the office to follow up on. Call me if you find anything of interest."

"Will do."

The detective got in in his vehicle and pulled away with a wave. Once the truck was gone, Sophie and Raveaux scanned the heavy undergrowth and the beach beyond.

"Well, now we have two and a half miles of coastal beach to search. How should we go about it?" Sophie said.

"Put yourself in the mind of the perps," Raveaux said. "They were carrying weapons. They would want to be somewhere concealed, but with easy entrance and exit in case they were confronted." He pointed to a narrow trail leading to the beach. "If I were camping, I'd pitch my tent on the beach and conceal it in the bushes. Maybe they were drinking to get in the mood. Perhaps lit a fire on the sand."

Sophie tugged down the brim of the HPD cap. "Let's get started."

2

Sophie and Raveaux made their way along the beach, searching for clues. They found several possible campsites, with disturbed sand patterns and buried fire rings, but nothing that told them anything that might be related to the bird killers.

Finally, about a mile from the beginning of the park, Sophie slid on a pair of latex gloves: she'd spotted a rusty tire iron protruding from an old fire ring. "What do you think? Seems like an odd place to discard this." She held up the tire iron for inspection.

Raveaux frowned. "You're right. Let's give this area a closer look."

They poked around, in and among the *naupaka* bushes, *ipomoea* vines, and beneath the umbrellalike branches of a beach heliotrope tree.

"I don't see anything more. What weapons did Kamuela say the killers used on the birds?" Sophie pulled her thick hair off her neck and twisted it up under the hat.

"A blade of some kind was used—a machete they think, and some kind of club," Raveaux said. "Your tire iron could be the club." Hands on his hips, the Frenchman stared at the fire ring thoughtfully. "Wouldn't you try to destroy a weapon that could tie you to the crime?"

"We're operating on the theory that the perps were kids because the headmaster of Kama'aina Schools is our client." Sophie fanned herself with a bit of cardboard she'd found. "Though we couldn't share that bit of info with Marcus Kamuela without our client's consent." She gazed longingly at the sea—if only she'd put her swimsuit on under her clothes that morning! "Since Dr. Ka'ula hired us and I wasn't at the intake meeting, was there anything specific he told you that might have tied Kama'aina students to the killing?"

"The headmaster was not forthcoming. Said he didn't want to open that can of worms until we found out if HPD would share the case with us. Now that Detective Kamuela has allowed us access, we need to meet with our client again and get whatever he knows." Raveaux stroked his chin. "If it was a couple of teens, they probably didn't realize how outraged the community—even the world, when the news got ahold of the story—was going to be."

"Let's dig deeper into this fire ring since there's nothing else in this area," Sophie said. "Maybe another weapon is buried deeper, and they were hoping fires built in this spot would eventually get rid of it."

"Sounds good." Raveaux unbuttoned his shirt and draped it over a bush. "No sense getting charcoal all over a perfectly good garment."

Sophie averted her eyes from Raveaux's leanly attractive, olive-skinned body. "It's so hot. I wish I could take my shirt off."

"Go ahead. I won't mind." Raveaux dropped to his knees beside her as she explored carefully inside the fire ring with latex covered gloves.

Sophie narrowed her eyes at Pierre over the rims of her sunglasses in a chastening squint. Raveaux hadn't asked one question, nor made any comment, about her relationship with Connor since she'd returned from her extended leave on Phi Ni. She'd been waiting for her reunion with her ex-boyfriend to come up.

One corner of Raveaux's stern mouth tucked in. "Don't worry. I've moved on. Heri Leede and I are dating."

"That's good. She's a fine match for you." Sophie released a breath, glad to put this awkward moment behind them. Raveaux had wanted to be more than friends since she'd met him; it was a bittersweet relief that he'd accepted her choice.

They dug carefully, removing pieces of semi-burned garbage and driftwood from the hole. Sophie felt something larger, flat, and long. She brushed the sand away.

"Look at this, Pierre." Sophie had located a molded plastic handle, halfway melted. She drew a short, lethal-looking, rust-covered machete out of the hole. "I think we found our murder weapon."

Raveaux got his phone out to call Kamuela. "No signal, but I picked up a voicemail from a blocked number." He frowned. "Can't retrieve it. We'll have to call at the parking lot."

"Let's go." Galvanized by the discovery, Sophie bagged the two items in a couple of paper evidence bags she'd had the foresight to bring. She swung her loaded backpack on and broke into a jog, enervating heat weariness dropping away.

Raveaux caught up, and they soon reached the parking lot where they'd left the white Security Solutions SUV.

When Sophie took her phone out, she too showed a blocked number. She listened to a short message from Connor asking her to call back immediately. She held the phone up for Raveaux to see. "Your call is probably Connor trying to reach us, too. It's likely about Pim Wat."

Raveaux's expression was carefully blank. "Should we call him back first, or Kamuela?"

"Let's get on the road to somewhere with a better signal. You call Kamuela while we drive, then let's return Connor's call together and see what he's concerned about."

"*Bien.*"

They got into the company SUV, taking a moment to refresh with bottles of water. Sophie turned on the vehicle while Raveaux called Kamuela to report their discovery. Hot air poured over them as the air-conditioning labored.

"Good work, you two. Can you bring the possible evidence in to the station? I'll meet you in the entrance area. I'd like to log the items into evidence right away," Kamuela's voice was rough with urgency after he'd listened to Raveaux's description. "I'll reach out to the District Attorney and schedule a meeting so we can clarify a legal process. Since this is an animal-related crime committed by humans, we need more direction on what to prioritize as far as building a prosecutable case. In the meantime, can you meet with your anonymous client and get more information? By then, we'll have plenty to discuss about the Moli Massacre and we can pull together a team meeting."

"Will do." Raveaux ended the call.

Sophie pulled the SUV into a convenient gas station and parked. "Let's reach out to Connor here, then take the evidence over to the HPD station." Sophie plugged the address of the downtown Honolulu Police Department location into the car's navigation system, barely taking a moment to notice the pretty tropical plantings around the gas station, and the comings and goings all around them.

Her heart rate had spiked since listening to the terse message from Connor.

He had to be calling about her deadly assassin mother. After all these months without a trace of Pim Wat, Sophie'd almost begun to relax and hope that the threat of retribution her mother had promised was over.

Raveaux had listened to his message as well. "Connor asks me to call back, too. Says it's important."

"Has to be about Pim Wat. No other reason he'd reach out to both of us like this." Sophie put her phone into a holder that held the display screen upright on the dash. "Let's use video. Ready?"

"Always." Raveaux's dark brown eyes twinkled; he almost smiled. Someday he'd smile more, and she hoped she'd be there to see it.

Sophie pressed an auto-programmed button to reach her lover, the mysterious cyber vigilante and Master of the Yām Khûmkạn in Thailand. As she listened to the pulse of signal for Connor to pick up, her gut clenched with both dread and anticipation.

Raveaux didn't look at the screen of the phone as it pulsed, ringing somewhere in a faraway jungle fortress; he gazed at Sophie's face.

She drew the eye, always, with something more than beauty. The ragged line of a scar earned on one of her cases bisected a high, tawny cheekbone and disappeared into her hairline, serving as an arrow pointing to her large eyes and full mouth.

Right now, those eyes were bright, and her lips pursed in a half-smile—she was eager to see the mysterious man in Thailand.

Not Raveaux, her loyal friend and colleague, godfather to her children.

Pierre Raveaux had lied.

He hadn't moved on from loving her.

But if Sophie knew how he felt, she'd distance herself, and that he couldn't bear.

"Sophie!" Wreathed in a smile, joy radiated from Connor's handsome face like sunlight as his image filled the screen.

The Master of the Yām Khûmkạn was different since Raveaux had seen him last. Happier. Healthier. More relaxed. That was Sophie's doing, most likely.

Jealousy was a cold blade to his heart.

"Hello, darling." Sophie was smiling, too. "Pierre is here, and we've got you on speakerphone. We were out investigating a new case together when we got your messages." She tilted the device politely so that Raveaux was included in the frame.

Raveaux made a little half wave. "*Bonjour.*"

"Ah, our French connection." The happiness that emanated from Connor's visage dimmed. "Glad you're there to keep an eye on Sophie and the kids. I appreciate it."

Raveaux bristled at the man's patronizing tone. He didn't respond.

Sophie glanced at Raveaux and frowned at the phone. "What's so urgent that you reached out to both of us in the middle of a workday?"

"It's your mother, of course, Sophie." Connor was all business as his eyes flicked down and to the left; Raveaux heard the rattle of a keyboard. "I've had surveillance attached to Kaleidoscope Tastemakers Ltd., that murder-for-hire front, ever since we found out about Pim Wat's relationship with their CEO, Enrique Mendoza. We haven't had so much as a glimpse of Pim Wat since she escaped Phi Ni months ago, but I think I found a hit she fulfilled for Mendoza—in Bali, of all places." He looked up and made eye contact with Pierre. "Raveaux, I want you to go to Bali and check out this lead."

3

Day 1

Lisabetta Scartuzzi walked along a stone-paved street, carrying a gilded shopping bag from a designer baby store. Lisabetta's white sundress caressed her freshly shaved legs; she enjoyed the way the breeze of her brisk strides blew air up her skirt, a sensual feeling.

Sunshine poured over her in an extravagant flood; she hid from it beneath a wide-brimmed straw hat. She loved the heat and light—had insisted, in fact, that her employer place her somewhere warm; even so, protecting her skin was a priority.

A workman on a scaffold, painting one of the buildings, paused mid-brushstroke to watch her pass; she smiled and waved, and the man almost fell off the ladder.

"It's the little things," Lisabetta murmured aloud, well-pleased. She might be a grandmother twice over, but she turned heads, and always would.

She reached the gate of her secure compound and keyed in a code that opened the side door beside a larger gate for cars. She took off her sunglasses and tipped her face up to the surveillance node so her guard could get a visual on her. Her newest face was reflected for a moment in the camera: wide cheekbones to match a wider jawline, with a pointed chin and full mouth. Her eyes and hair were a new color; even her skin was lighter, thanks to nightly applications of a bleaching solution.

She was no longer Pim Wat; she was Lisabetta now, and she was enjoying a new, softer personality to go with her looks.

Lisabetta blew a kiss with a smile to her guard; Pim Wat would never have done that.

Inside the wall, she relaxed her shoulders and surveyed the pretty garden borders that surrounded the parking courtyard before her house's elegant entrance. The place was a rental, but perfect for her purposes. Finding and outfitting it had taken months after an extensive search. She'd had it made over to Lisabetta's tastes—and on one suite, she'd lavished extra care and attention.

After greeting her housekeeper, hanging up her hat, and accepting a glass of cool ice water with a slice of lemon, Lisabetta clicked her way on designer sandals up the tiled steps to the second floor. She turned left and headed down the hall to the children's room, still holding the shopping bag.

Once in the doorway, she paused to evaluate: had she duplicated everything correctly to match the latest video of the nursery at her daughter's house in Kailua?

The wall colors were perfect: one side a pale lavender for the girl, the other a tender aqua blue for the baby boy. Their beds were duplicated right down to the choice of sheets. Across the room, shelves of books and bins of their favorite, familiar toys were in place. The colorful throw rug in the middle of the room, with its circular pattern of alphabet letters, was the same; the changing table for the baby was equipped to the last identical detail.

Lisabetta walked over to that changing table and reached inside the gilded bag.

Finding baby Sean's favorite rattle had been a chore way out here in this corner of the world; she'd had to work with the fancy baby store to get the thing ordered. Now, she set the rattle on the changing table at an inviting angle and turned from there to gaze at the room.

Everything was ready for her grandchildren.

It was time to execute her plan to bring them to live with her permanently.

4

Important note for those following both series:
Sophie's Paradise Crime Thrillers take place in the five-year gap between Rip Tides #9 and Bone Hook #10 in the Lei's Paradise Crime Mystery timeline, so Lei's perspective will reflect that.

Day 1

Lei swiveled her office chair restlessly, tapping one of the department issue Bic ballpoint pens against her teeth as she read a message forwarded to her through the Maui Police Department's e-mail server.

> "Dear MPD: please, please do something to help us find out who has stolen three eggs from the endangered Laysan albatross (moli) sanctuary here on Maui! We have reported the crime, but no one seems to be taking it seriously. These birds are sacred to the Hawaiian people as 'aumakua, and we have fought hard to create a nesting sanctuary out near Waihee for them, investing in buying the coastal land they historically nest in and fencing out feral cats and mongooses so the chicks can

hatch—but that wasn't enough, as recent events unfortunately show. We need to find out what happened to these priceless eggs, before the few birds we've coaxed to settle here give up coming to Maui altogether.
Considering the recent massacre on Oahu, MPD's support is more important than ever.
Please help the moli!
Sincerely,
Dr. Danica Powers
Vice President and Chief Biologist, Albatross Sanctuary Maui"

Attached to the e-mail, at the bottom, was a photo of a pair of albatrosses. Their graceful necks were crossed to make a heart shape as they gazed down with obvious grief and loss at an empty nest.

"Oh, that's just mean," Lei muttered. "Ow. My heart." She scrolled to the top of the e-mail but couldn't find a sender for the forward—it had been blind copied from someone else's computer at the station.

Lei and her partner Pono Kaihale's cubicle in the main open area of the building was cluttered, as were all the modular units filling the room. A bulletin board occupied one moveable wall on each side of their old-fashioned computers.

On her bulletin board, Lei had indulged in a small mosaic of family photos that included herself, her husband Stevens, their five-year-old son Kiet, and portraits of their two Rottweilers, Keiki and Conan. An old snapshot of Lei as a teenager with her beloved Auntie Rosario, along with a recent one of her father Wayne and her grandfather Soga, rounded out the collage.

The rest of the corkboard was taken up with wanted posters and news alerts from the Department, per regulations.

Pono's entire corner, in contrast, was papered with his children Maile and Ikaika's soccer team photos—both kids were stars in the sport. He'd also given his entire bulletin board over to family snapshots of his statuesque wife Tiare, and the family together.

"Of course, he's counting on me to keep track of all the departmental bulletins," Lei muttered. She wasn't irritated, though; she and Pono had a functional and solid working relationship they had maintained for years. "When one falls down, the other can pick them up," was a perfect way to summarize their sibling like relationship.

Lei set down the chewed-on Bic and got up to fetch another cup of coffee. Usually, Pono brought her a mug of the department's strong black brew, but she'd have to get her own today; her partner was out speaking at a middle school about the part police officers play in keeping the community safe.

The employee lounge was empty when Lei found her favorite chipped MPD mug and filled it from the community pot. She dumped in a teaspoon of powdered creamer, stirring vigorously so that the chunks dissolved. "When are they going to fix that good coffee maker Sophie bought us?" Lei mused aloud.

"It's not actually broken. I put it away because those damn coffee pods are too expensive." Her boss, Lieutenant CJ Omura, spoke from behind Lei, making her jump.

"Can't we do a fundraiser or something? Having a good cup of coffee really improves my job performance." Lei lofted the mug, sniffing audibly. "This stuff literally stinks."

"I welcome any and all outside donations to that worthy cause." Omura took down her own mug. "Show me the money."

"Speaking of worthy causes . . ." Lei turned to face her boss . . . "I got a sad e-mail from the biologist at the Maui Albatross Sanctuary begging for help with their investigation into three missing live eggs. I was wondering . . ."

"No." Omura clanked her mug down on the counter with a bang. "I've already heard about that case, and the answer is no. We have way too many human-related crimes going on to steal resources for something like that. The sanctuary nonprofit has deep pockets. They can afford to pay for a private investigator who will have quality time to dedicate to the mystery of the missing eggs." Omura splashed coffee into her cup; she was agitated, because some spilled on her immaculate dress pants. She swore and scrubbed at the spot with a paper napkin. "Now look what you made me do."

"You're just bummed because we don't have the manpower to help," Lei said boldly. Years of working with Omura had given her insight into the intimidating "Steel Butterfly" and her boss's well-hidden soft heart. "You know how I feel about endangered birds. Please let me take this on. I promise I'll work it during my off-hours."

"When do you have any off-hours? I recently reviewed your last month's overtime log, and I don't want you lying on that report when you've got a kid at home to take care of. The answer is no, and that's final." Omura stomped out of the lounge, her fancy heels clacking on the lounge's tiled floor.

Lei stared into her mug thoughtfully. Chunks of powdered creamer were still floating in it, refusing to melt. She procured a wooden stir stick and squashed at them.

She was not at all surprised by Omura's dictum, nor was she deterred by it.

The *moli* needed her help, and they were going to get it. She had been outraged, as had so many of the public, by the terrible attack on the sacred birds at their Kaʻena Point refuge on Oahu. If there was even a ghost of a chance that the two cases were connected, Lei wanted to be the one to find the link . . . and break it.

"With my bare hands, if necessary." Lei tossed the wooden stirrer into the compostable recycling; that bin and other innovations were new, and due to Omura's advocacy within the department.

Her boss cared about the environment and its creatures, but Omura was right. Lei and Pono had too many cases they were making little progress on, cases that involved loss of human lives.

Lei's friend Sophie Smithson would be interested in this case, though, and she was a private investigator. Maybe the Albatross Sanctuary could afford to hire her . . . and in any case, reaching out to Sophie would be a good way to find out if there was anything online connecting the theft of missing, live albatross eggs to Oahu's Moli Massacre.

Lei was long overdue for a chat with her friend, anyway. She headed back to her cubicle with a new spring to her steps.

5

Day 1

Connor, Master of the Yām Khûmkạn, sat before his bank of monitors in the tower room of the jungle fortress. He addressed Devin McDonald, his contact with the CIA, in the video monitor. "I have a new lead on the assassin Pim Wat," he said. "I'd like to review our amnesty deal in case I have to leave the country in pursuit of her."

"Can't give you any protection outside of Thailand." McDonald shook his head and his florid jowls jiggled. "Not gonna fly. The task force has agreed not to touch you there, but that's the extent of our agreement until you fulfill your end of the bargain."

"The bargain" had been drafted between Connor and the international task force that had been pursuing him for online vigilante activities. The group, consisting of CIA, Secret Service, and Interpol, had agreed that if Connor found and detained Pim Wat and turned her over to them, he would have clemency and freedom.

But Pim Wat had spectacularly evaded them not long ago. The task force had been humiliated by the failed operation, and they needed a scapegoat.

Connor suppressed his raging frustration; his private island of

Phi Ni off the coast of Thailand remained the only refuge where he and Sophie could meet until this nightmare was resolved.

"I'll be sending a team to follow up on this lead, then. The destination is Bali," Connor said.

"Keep me informed. I have a contact in the islands you can liaise with over there." They exchanged details. McDonald cut the connection with the jab of a fat finger.

"Jerk," Connor muttered. He shut his eyes as the familiar feeling of being trapped engulfed him. As the Master of the Yām Khûmkạn, Thailand's equivalent of the CIA, Connor was now one of the most powerful men in Asia; but he was stuck in a stone tower in the middle of the jungle like some freakin' Rapunzel without a rope.

A knock came from the door—one short knock, two long—the code his personal attendant used. Four was a young and ambitious graduate of the Yām Khûmkạn's ninja training program whose designation of Four Hundred Forty-Three Connor'd finally had to learn, and shorten, after his faithful friend Nine's death. "Enter."

Four entered, carrying a tray. "Your supper, Master."

The Thai man had a bright magenta aura shot through with yellow rays. An exemplary warrior and clearly intelligent, Nine had groomed and chosen Four to fulfill the position of caring for Connor's needs for a reason—but Nine hadn't had enough time before his death to share that reason.

Connor studied the young ninja as he set out the meal on the room's table.

There was nothing outwardly objectionable about the man's appearance or his behavior—except that Connor hadn't wanted a personal attendant. Hadn't wanted anyone to get close to him again —anyone who did could be used as a weapon, and then the loss would never stop hurting—as Nine's continued to do.

Connor's life was full of these dilemmas. Attempts to protect himself always seemed to fail; that was not lost on him.

Still, there was no room for anyone to replace Nine at Connor's side. "Leave the food on the table and go."

Four unloaded the tray and carefully arranged the covered bowls, utensils, tea-things and napkin. He hesitated a long moment, then padded out. The door closed softly behind him.

Connor got up and went to the portal. He dropped the heavy wooden bar into the stanchions on either side of the door, locking it.

Four, who waited outside guarding him, couldn't fail to hear Connor's rejection.

Connor felt a guilty twinge; he was being a jerk, too.

He'd been doing that a lot since Nine died, and after he'd had to say goodbye to Sophie.

Connor returned to the table and lifted the ceramic cover off a steaming bowl of curried rice, meat, and vegetables that Four would have taste-tested for poisons. He picked up his chopsticks and gazed out the single window of the tower as he ate, meditatively watching the martial arts drilling of the men in the courtyard far below.

Connor's thoughts wandered back to the call with Sophie and Raveaux.

He should have been more courteous to the man who was Sophie's trusted friend and the godfather of her children, but he'd been patronizing and curt, ordering Raveaux to prepare to travel to Bali to follow up on Pim Wat, though he was less sure than the last time that the lead would pan out.

The connection was slim: only a mention in the Balinese news that a businessman known to have mob connections had mysteriously died in his sleep, and authorities were searching for a "petite blonde woman" who'd been spotted on closed circuit TV leaving the man's chambers.

Connor had hacked into the authorities' evidence file and reviewed the footage. The possible killer's face hadn't been visible in the CCTV, but she'd been the right size, dressed as a prostitute wearing a long blonde wig, Pim Wat's modus operandi—and something about the quick, graceful way the woman moved rang true.

Wasn't much, but he was sending Raveaux out anyway.

Could his decision be a little like King David sending Bathsheba's husband to the front lines to be killed?

"Raveaux gets to see Sophie and the kids anytime he wants, while

I'm stuck here," Connor muttered. Without his friend Nine to talk to, the empty room had become his confessional.

Connor pushed his half-finished meal away. This dark mood and his rude behavior—both were beneath him. He was the Master, and his title called for a higher standard—but Connor was just a jealous fool half a world away from his beloved.

The solution lay not in treating those beneath him poorly, but in finding Pim Wat and turning her over to the authorities. Once that was done, Connor could make a home with Sophie in the United States, or here in Thailand. Hell, anywhere in the world; the whole planet was their playground.

"I need to focus on replacing myself here at the Yām Khûmkạn. The men aren't yet ready to do without me." Connor'd been restructuring the organization, building subgroup democracies among the diverse disciplines and departments.

This had worked to a degree, but the culture of the ancient organization was rigidly hierarchical. The men were used to a dictatorship, and Connor was trying to build egalitarianism; the changeover wasn't going quickly. He would work on it every day; then, no matter how stalled the search for Pim Wat was, he'd be moving toward his goal: freedom to be with Sophie, somewhere far from here.

Connor got up and went to the door. He lifted the heavy bar and opened it, peering out.

Four, seated cross-legged against the wall, bounded to his feet. "Yes, Master?"

"I want you to go and fetch the teacher leaders of all the disciplines. Tell them to meet me in the outdoor courtyard near the tiger's-eye column."

"Yes, Master!" The young man turned to go with alacrity.

"And Four . . ."

The ninja's brown eyes gleamed with intelligence as he gazed back at Connor, waiting. His new assistant had an irrepressible, resilient presence and a strong, positive aura; perhaps that's what Nine had seen in him. Who knew how long this situation would go on? Connor couldn't risk becoming someone he hated while he hoped for an uncertain future.

"What's your name? I mean, what was it, before you joined the Yām Khûmkạn?" Connor asked.

"Feirn." The man's brows drew together in puzzlement.

"So—Fern? Like the plant?"

"Yes." Feirn seemed confused by the personal question and attention; he ducked his head and stared at his feet.

"Well, I'll be calling you by Feirn from now on in private. Okay?"

"Yes." Feirn met Connor's gaze cautiously. "And what is your name, Master?"

Connor didn't suppress the smile that broke across his face—Feirn was brave as well as bright. "My name is Connor."

An answering grin split the young man's face. "I am pleased to serve you, Connor." He spun and ran down the stairs on light feet.

Connor stared after Feirn; it was worth the risk of a human connection to be a little less lonely—or at least, he hoped so.

6

Day 2

The next morning, Sophie sat down at the small table inside her Security Solutions downtown office with operative Lono Jones. Their new client, Dr. Ka'ula, the headmaster of Kama'aina Schools, was soon scheduled to call in for a video conference regarding the Moli Massacre case.

Sunshine pierced the glare resistant windows. The tinting was inadequate; the room was still too bright for Sophie, tired as she was from getting up several times during the night with fussy Sean.

She set her tablet aside and stood. "I'm going to fix a cup of tea. Would you like some?"

Jones glanced at her from hazel eyes beneath thick blond brows. "Sorry. I don't think your tea station has been refilled since you went out on leave. I'm a coffee kinda guy."

"Oh, of course." Jones had been using her office for the last six months as he covered her maternity leave; no surprise the tea station wasn't restocked. "I'll let Paula know."

Sophie walked around to the front of her desk, still littered with Jones's personal items: a ball made of rubber bands, a tiny replica sniper rifle complete with stand, a much-battered paper blotter calendar marked with coffee stains, a Marine Corps mug.

"I also haven't had time to get my shit out of your desk," Jones said. "Sorry."

Jones didn't sound sorry; he sounded put upon.

"My return date wasn't exactly a surprise, Mr. Jones." Sophie said, annoyed.

"Really? Mr. Jones?" The former Maui Police Department detective pushed a hand through disordered blond locks that looked like they'd dried in the wind as he came in from surfing. "I think we're getting off on the wrong foot. Call me Lono, at least."

"And you may call me Sophie." She swept a crumpled paper cup out of the way and pressed the call button. "Paula? Can you come refresh the beverage station? And box up Mr. Jones's things and take them to his desk, wherever that is."

"Sure, Sophie. I should have thought of that. On my way!" As always, Paula's upbeat cheer was a mood lifter.

The monitor for the upcoming meeting chimed with a call just as dapper Kendall Bix, President of Operations, pushed open the door and stepped inside.

"Perfect timing." Bix held an electronic tablet under his arm as well as a manila folder; the company tried to be entirely paperless, but a paper trail always seemed to proliferate. At times, Sophie preferred the relative security of paper; old-school case files couldn't be hacked. The client in the Moli Massacre case had asked for paper records only, and Sophie was interested to know why.

Her assistant Paula followed Bix in, pushing a cart loaded with refreshment supplies for the credenza. Meanwhile, Jones answered the incoming call from Headmaster Ka'ula.

Soon the three Security Solutions people were seated at the round table while Paula quietly worked in the background.

"We are able to liaise with the Honolulu Police Department, specifically Detective Marcus Kamuela, assigned to the Moli Massacre." Sophie opened the meeting after greeting the headmaster, a self-important Hawaiian man she'd met on a previous case. "In return, we're expected to share any and all evidence we gather on this crime with HPD. I'm hoping to hear in detail what inspired you to engage our services, Dr. Ka'ula."

The middle-aged headmaster wore a perpetual frown and his dark brown eyes seemed to hide under a wedge of black brows. "What do you mean, share any and all evidence with HPD?"

Bix tapped the table with a pen. "Come now, Dr. Ka'ula. You asked us, in our original meeting, to see what we could find out from the police. Surely you didn't think that was a one-way information street? Otherwise, we would just engage in our own investigation and get as far as we could with it confidentially—an entirely different process."

Ka'ula's full lips pursed. "I wanted to know what they know."

"Of course," Sophie said, stifling growing irritation. "But that's not how cooperation works. On the outing we took with Detective Kamuela to the crime scene, I discovered possible evidence and I turned it over to the police per protocol."

"You did what?" Ka'ula unbuttoned the top button of a dressy aloha shirt; his neck was mottled with angry color. "This is a disaster."

"I'm sure you aren't suggesting that we suppress evidence pertinent to the case," Sophie said icily. "Especially something as important as a possible weapon used in the killings."

Ka'ula groaned aloud. "Tell me what the hell you found."

Sophie missed Pierre Raveaux acutely in that moment; Raveaux had been good at calming reactivity in clients. Raveaux was off the case, though, preparing to go to Bali to hunt for her mother, and Jones had been assigned to replace him. Jones had been silent thus far, but he was taking notes on a tiny laptop, tanned fingers flying.

Sophie described the tire iron and rusty machete that she and Raveaux had uncovered. "Bix has included photos in your confidential file. Would you like me to share them remotely?"

"No. I don't want anything about the case to get out, anywhere."

"I think it's time you told us why you engaged this agency in the first place," Bix inserted smoothly. "And clarify if you want us to continue to work with the police or conduct a private investigation on our own."

Sophie glanced at Bix sharply. She'd called upon her personal relationship with Marcus Kamuela in order to get access to the case and its records. Withdrawing cooperation now would burn Marcus, and she likely wouldn't be able to ask favors of him in the future.

But Ka'ula hung his head. "This can't ever come back to me, or I'd be crucified by the parents and the board." He scrubbed a hand over his face. "But I couldn't sit on what I'd heard without doing something. All I ask is that you help mitigate the damage if the killers turn out to be our students."

"Of course, Dr. Ka'ula. You're our client. Your interests and confidentiality are our priority," Bix soothed.

Jones bent over, making a gagging sound of contempt out of view of the camera. "Excuse me. I need some water." The lanky ex-detective got up and went to the freshly restocked tea station on the credenza, reaching for the carafe.

Sophie liked Jones more in that moment than she had thus far.

"Ahem," the headmaster harrumphed. "Three months ago, when the attack on the albatrosses happened, we heard rumors at the school. Different teachers overheard snippets of conversation and so on. They came to me. That's why I reached out to you, worried about the—the crime. Then—since Ms. Smithson wasn't available and I had confidence in her expertise—I rescinded the request for help."

"Did you decide it wasn't worth pursuing?" Bix asked gently. "That you didn't have enough for an investigation?"

"No. Frankly, I was hoping the whole thing would blow over. But it didn't. Instead, outrage built with the public." Ka'ula shook his head mournfully. "I wanted Ms. Smithson because I trust her skill after another sensitive case we had with you folks." He squinted into the camera as if searching for something. "Where's Mr. Raveaux? He's good. We worked well together."

"Monsieur Raveaux is on another assignment," Bix replied. "You met Lono Jones earlier. He will be taking Raveaux's place as Sophie's partner in the field."

Jones set a mug of Thai tea, trailing a string with a tag, in front of Sophie. She gave him a quick smile of thanks. Jones resumed his seat and lifted his cup, marked with the Security Solutions logo, in a toast. "Pierre leaves some big shoes to fill, but I'll do my best."

"Dr. Ka'ula. Why don't you tell us the rumors the teachers shared, specifically?" Sophie wrapped her fingers around the hot beverage to warm them. "And any social media leads you might have. I'm guessing that's how the students were communicating."

"Yes, indeed." Ka'ula smoothed his shirtfront as if petting a nervous animal. "The rumors were that two of the students did the killing as—as a kind of hazing ritual. There's a secret club they were being inducted into. That app with the disappearing photos was involved."

Sophie named several apps with that feature, and Ka'ula nodded at the one that was most used by teenagers, a site where photos dissolved after being viewed. "Apparently pictures of the killings, and eggs that were taken and not destroyed, were posted to prove the task was completed. As time went by and the publicity became virulent against whoever had killed the birds, gossip went quiet on the subject. However, one of our security staff poses as a student on social media to monitor for cyberbullying and got a screenshot that might be evidence. I'll send it to Ms. Smithson's phone."

"Can I get the identity and login information for the security agent's student account?" Sophie asked. "Have your staffer give it over to me for the duration of the investigation, and I'll use that to find out whatever I can."

"Of course," Ka'ula said. "In the meantime, here's the photo."

Sophie braced herself as her phone dinged with an incoming message.

The picture was innocuous enough; a large, speckled albatross egg rested in a cardboard box atop cloth padding. An adjacent lightbulb provided warmth. "What is this?"

She punted the photo to the group, and it appeared on the monitor beside Ka'ula's image.

"The perps only broke a few eggs. They stole the rest," Ka'ula said. "My security staffer thinks they sold them on the Internet."

"This is time-sensitive information that you should have taken to the police." Anger prickled the skin of Sophie's neck and chest.

The big man lowered his head to glare from beneath his heavy brows. "Do you have any idea how bad it would be for the school if it came out publicly that our students were involved in this crime against helpless endangered birds?"

"You want us to help you cover up what we find." Jones spoke with deadly calm. "Because that would be better for the school's image."

"That's why I'm hiring you, yes. I'm hoping to find answers *and* find a way to mitigate the damage." Ka'ula opened his hands toward them in a gesture of appeal. "I'm not asking you to cover anything up. Just to help . . . soften what you might find."

"Well, that's a lot of what we do at Security Solutions." Bix glared meaningfully at Jones. "You are our client, Dr. Ka'ula, and your concerns are our concerns, as I said before."

Sophie folded her lips into a line, squeezing her hot mug forcefully. This job wasn't going to be one of the easy ones.

※

Alone at last after the long day, dinner done and the kids in bed with Armita to monitor them, Sophie settled herself in front of the three monitors she maintained at her new house in Kailua. She'd moved her family there shortly after Sean's birth, in large part because it was more secure than the Pendragon Arches apartment in downtown Honolulu where she'd lived for years. Decorated in a minimalist palette of cool grays with the sound-baffling carpet she liked for such workspaces, her office was a sensory oasis from the chaos of family and dogs.

Sophie's computer rigs, Jinjai, Amara, and Ying, hummed into life at the touch of a button on her key fob. Sophie took the moments as they booted up to go over to the exercise station in the corner of the room and engage in pull-ups. She was a believer in the maintenance of consistent environments and habits; these created greater ease and effectiveness in compartmentalizing her life.

But not today.

As Sophie hung with extended arms from the high steel bar, her mind ticked through the day's events: the meeting at the office with Ka'ula and Bix's lecture afterward on the priorities of a private security firm being customer service over actual results—a message that left a bad taste in both Sophie's and Jones's mouths after careers in public service. After that wrangle, she'd met alone with Jones to divide up tasks as they moved ahead with the investigation.

She'd left her new partner to review the case records Kamuela had shared, as well as the surveillance footage from the crime scene, materials she'd already perused.

The bombshell Ka'ula had revealed about the eggs possibly being viable was one she wanted to pass on to Kamuela, but she'd run out of time to do anything more on the case that day—she'd had to come home to take Sean to a well-baby appointment.

The good news was Sean was hitting all his growth milestones at the 90th percentile. The bad news was that he'd needed some immunization shots—likely, she was in for another rough night.

Sophie flexed and dragged her body up to the bar, able to hook her chin briefly over it, but was only able to complete six full reps.

"*Effluent of a flatulent pig!*" Sophie exclaimed in frustration as she dropped to the ground. Her arms were not what they used to be. She stepped from the padded rubber mat that marked the workout area to grab a ten-pound weight.

Back at the desk, she was ready to settle into searching for activity online regarding the albatross atrocities. Using one hand to type and the other to curl the weight, she activated her rogue data mining program, DAVID (Data Analysis Victim Information Database), on the Jinjai rig.

Sophie typed in search parameters with keywords related to the case, widening to include photos, videos, and art or graphic illustrations. She switched the weight to the other hand, doing bicep curls as she activated her second rig. She then opened windows and arranged social media apps on the monitor so she could see several at once.

Sophie slowly raised and lowered the weight as she perused the many posts, memes and bits of video sprinkled with dialog that cycled through diversified feeds. The American teenage social media scene felt as strange as entering a bar in the Star Wars universe: language, clothing, and even their appearance made it a foreign world.

She needed to coordinate with the security officer that had created the accounts and get help interpreting what she was reading and seeing.

Sophie sent a quick text to Jones, asking him to track down the headmaster and punt her the staffer's contact info. She'd get that person's take on the situation directly rather than going through Ka'ula.

In the meantime, she and Jones had an early meeting the next morning at the Honolulu Police Department headquarters with Kamuela and District Attorney Chang to go over the best way to build a prosecutable case in a situation that involved crimes against endangered species.

DAVID was working, sifting the Internet for her. She might as well call it a night and grab some rest while she could.

Day 3

At a stoplight on her way to the downtown HPD meeting with Marcus Kamuela and the District Attorney the next morning, Sophie flipped down the sunshade of her older Lexus SUV and added a pop of lipstick to brighten her sallow face. As she'd worried, Sean had been up several times the night before and she wasn't feeling or looking her best.

On the seat beside her, Sophie's phone toned with an incoming call; Sophie picked up for Lei Texeira, her friend in the Maui Police Department.

"Lei! It's been too long since we've talked."

"Hey, Sophie. I wish I was calling to catch up, but I'm reaching out about a case." Her friend's voice held the lilt of a native of the Hawaiian islands. "I heard from Marcus that you've picked up a private gig related to the albatross case."

Sophie's attention sharpened, though she continued to navigate the busy Honolulu commute traffic with aplomb. "I have, as a matter of fact. Though technically I'm not supposed to say anything—unless you're working with Marcus on it?"

"I am. I just got off the phone with him."

"Oh. Well then—may I ask what your interest is?"

"Sure." Lei's tone went brisk. "We've had a crime here on Maui that resembles the atrocity on Oahu. Someone broke into the albatross's fenced nesting sanctuary here on Maui and stole the eggs of several nesting albatross pairs."

"Foul stench of a rotting corpse!" Sophie exclaimed. "I was planning to share some relevant new info with the whole team at this morning's meeting. Is there any way you can call in and join the meeting then?"

"Sure, absolutely. Put me on speaker or video when the group is together," Lei said. "Now that we've got that out of the way, how're things with you?"

Sophie brushed breakfast crumbs off the breast of the red tunic top she'd put on that morning, hoping for a little of her former body confidence. "Sean had shots yesterday and a very bad night last night. Otherwise, fine."

"Marcella tells me you're back together with the mystery man from Thailand?"

"Yes. I never really stopped being in love with Connor." Warmth bloomed in Sophie's cheeks as she remembered last night's call to Connor as Sean fussed on her shoulder; his loving and sexy encouragement had got her through several sleepless hours with an

37

unhappy baby. "I'm not enjoying having a long-distance relationship, though. We've been apart for years now, but once we reconnected romantically, everything changed."

"Are you sure . . ."

"Please don't question my choice, Lei. I'm getting very tired of other people's opinions," Sophie snapped.

Lei was silent for a moment. "That wasn't what I was going to ask," her friend eventually said. "I was going to ask if you were sure his legal problems would all be resolved when your mother was imprisoned."

Sophie guided the car down a ramp into the underground parking garage at HPD. "I hope so. I believe so," she said at last. "Connor has promised to give up—that other thing too, to be with me." Sophie never put his vigilantism into words that could be overheard. "He'll be working with intelligence here in the US once Pim Wat is taken into custody."

"Well, great." Her friend's voice was infused with fake enthusiasm. "I'll be waiting for your call in to the meeting. Talk soon!" Lei hung up.

"*Sweet son of a goatherd.*" Sophie pulled into a visitor parking stall, deflated. Couldn't even one of her friends or family be happy that she and Connor were together again?

The HPD conference room was a utilitarian space whose walls were ringed with whiteboards. A large, elaborate brass medallion inscribed with the state motto was mounted on the wall overlooking a podium, currently moved aside.

Sophie took a seat at the battered Formica table, surprised to see that Lono Jones had arrived before her. "Hello, partner."

"Hey." The blond man combed his shoulder-length hair back with his fingers; water dampened the shoulders of a wrinkled aloha shirt he wore with jeans. He'd set a cup of McDonald's coffee on the table beside the stack of files she'd given him to review. "Thought I'd beat you to it and have a few more minutes with the file."

"I thought I'd get here early, too, but we just made it in time. Traffic." She yawned unexpectedly.

"Babies wake up?" Jones might appear laid-back, but his hazel eyes were observant.

"Yes. Four times." Another yawn startled Sophie. "Excuse me. I need more stimulant than one cup of tea."

"Here." Jones pushed his cup of coffee over. "Haven't touched it yet."

"Thank you." Sophie never drank coffee, but this was an emergency. She took a tentative sip. The stuff was hot and tasted burnt—and that alone woke her up. "Did you get that login info for me?"

Jones dug in his pocket and handed a Post-it note over to her. "I got you a phone number. The client wants you to call his security staffer direct."

"Okay. That's best, anyway."

Sophie was halfway through the cup of terrible coffee when District Attorney Alan Chang came in with Marcus Kamuela in his wake. Chang was a short, slender man dressed in a muted aloha shirt and chinos, otherwise known as Hawaii business casual. Friendly-looking crinkles bracketed intelligent, calculating eyes.

"Where's Raveaux?" Kamuela asked.

"He had an urgent assignment that took him out of the country," Sophie said. "This is Lono Jones, formerly a detective with Maui Police Department, and our new associate. Jones, this is HPD Detective Marcus Kamuela and District Attorney Alan Chang."

The men shook hands.

Chang addressed Sophie. "Glad you could make it on short notice," he said. "Detective Kamuela asked to have a team meeting to make sure we are all on the same page going forward. This case has garnered much public attention."

Sophie cleared her throat. "On that note, I came across some new information I need to share. Sergeant Lei Texeira called me from Maui as I was on my way here." She met Kamuela's eyes. "I asked if she could call in so I could share the intel with everyone at once."

Kamuela glanced at Chang. "Texeira is a colleague and friend, a detective sergeant on Maui. She contacted me yesterday, as well. They've had a crime against the albatross on their island that has a lot in common with the Moli Massacre, and she'd like to get in on our discussion."

"She can join via conference call," the DA agreed.

Kamuela pulled a three-sided speakerphone out of a cubbyhole under the podium and plugged it in, looking up Lei's number on his cell phone and dialing it. A few minutes later, Lei's voice spoke. "Sergeant Texeira, Maui Police Department."

"Lei, it's Marcus. I'm calling from our team meeting." Kamuela identified the people present and the location. "Sophie wants to start us off with some new intel."

"Yes." Sophie faced the speakerphone and spoke clearly. "First of all, I have our client's permission to be identified. We were hired by the headmaster of Kama'aina Schools, Dr. Ka'ula." She waited a beat for that to sink in and then went on, filling them in on the background that had brought Ka'ula to their doors. "He was reluctant to go to the police directly because he . . ." she paused, groping for words.

"He knew how bad it would look that some of his students might have committed this crime," Kamuela growled. "And I'm guessing he wants us to whitewash that for the public."

"We explained that wasn't possible," Sophie said. "Though he asked that we try to keep it out of the news." Both Chang and Kamuela stared at her expressionlessly.

Sophie forged on. "In the course of reviewing students' social media, it's come to light that the perps, who might have killed the birds in a hazing or loyalty testing ritual, didn't destroy all the eggs. They sold some of them on the Internet." Sophie shunted the picture of the egg in the box to Kamuela to be stored in the case file.

"And that's why I'm calling," Lei said, her voice echoing in the room through the speaker. "We've had a theft of three albatross eggs here on Maui. The birds only lay one egg per year, so the loss is a big deal."

"This opens up a whole new avenue to investigate," Kamuela agreed, moving his muscular shoulders restlessly. "But who the hell would buy an albatross egg? And how could it be shipped anywhere without it dying?"

"Don't know the answers to those questions," Jones said. "But I agree it gives us more of an avenue to explore. Sergeant Texeira, do you have any leads?"

"No. There's a nonprofit that's dedicated to the birds' survival on this island; they paid to fence conservation grounds near Waihee to keep out the feral cats and mongooses so the birds could nest unmolested," Lei said. "The group monitors the birds closely, but they don't use surveillance cameras. They were the ones to call in the missing eggs and ask for help. Normally it's not the kind of case I would get; I work in homicide. But I have an interest in endangered birds and I was upset when I heard about the Moli Massacre on Oahu. It worries me that it might have sparked something related over here. Now that I know eggs were stolen on Oahu, too, it seems like there's a connection."

They reviewed the little gleaned so far from the surveillance video and trips out to the desecrated area.

"We speculated the perps might have camped there in order to have easier access for their raid, and that's how I found the tire iron and machete that might have been used in the attack. Have your people found any forensic evidence on the tools?" Sophie asked.

"They're in the queue to be analyzed," Kamuela said. "We're backed up a couple of weeks, unfortunately. You have a background in tech, Sophie. Can you take charge of the tech aspects of the case?" Kamuela asked. "I've been assigned several new homicides, so I'd like to pass the baton as much as I can."

"I assumed as much," Sophie said. "I've already got several areas to follow up on." She took a breath. "Mr. Chang, what kind of legal ramifications will there be if the killers are underage? What kind of consequences would you go for?"

The DA frowned. "I was already concerned that we won't have much of a legal precedent for prosecution, and that problem will be amplified if the perps are minors. Animal rights laws notoriously lack teeth, even for adult perpetrators of abuse. The public might be howling for blood, but getting anything to stick to minors will be that much harder. We will have to protect their confidentiality, as well."

Marcus Kamuela smacked his hands down on the table in a gesture of frustration that made everyone jump. "Well, until we have more to go on, I've got to roll. My partner's waiting and we've got murderers to catch."

Out at the parking lot, Sophie turned to Jones. "I need to work out before I sit down to more hours in front of a computer. I like a gym called Fight Club—I used to do some MMA there back in the day. Care to join me?"

Jones's blond brows rose. "To spar?"

Sophie shook her head. "No. I've lost my taste for the ring. But I still like to use their workout area."

"Nah, I'm not a gym guy. Unless you consider the ocean a gym." Jones smiled. "I went surfing earlier this morning, so I'm good to go. What can I get started on?"

"Why don't you reach out to the Kama'aina Schools contact you got for me and set up a meeting for us? Then, get ahold of Lei and find out more about this group that advocates for the albatross. See if they have any leads on people who might want to steal the eggs, anything that might connect our cases. The rest of what I need to do is a bunch of work online. I'll probably work from home because I need to use some specialized programs I have on the computers there."

"Gotcha, boss. See you back at the office, or wherever." Jones gave a two-fingered salute, turned, and strode away.

Sophie got into the Lexus to head to her old haunt, Fight Club.

So much had taken place in that barn-like building with the dangling lights that formed pools of illumination over the sparring ring and fitness equipment lining the walls. Fight Club was where she'd really begun to heal from the physical and emotional abuse her ex-husband had inflicted during her early, terrible marriage.

Fight Club was also where she'd met Alika Wolcott, her coach and Momi's father—and for that alone, the gym would always be a special place. She and Alika continued as close friends, co-parenting Momi as effectively as they could. Today, Fight Club would just be a place to pound some weights and get rid of frustration left over from the meeting.

Sophie pressed down on the accelerator as she pulled out of the downtown parking lot.

No matter how hard they tried to build a case, the team might not be able to punish these killers in any conventional way, and that didn't sit well with Sophie.

7

Day 3

Pierre Raveaux rolled his least heavy trousers tightly, smoothing them so they wouldn't wrinkle, and tucked them into the lightweight carry-on bag he used for international travel. Checking a bag was fraught with the risk of missing luggage, and he didn't want to take that chance, especially heading for an unknown place like Indonesia.

His adolescent kitten, Lisette, pounced on the carry-on from behind the pillow on the bed. She lashed her striped, gray tail, her paws splayed, and butt raised; her antics startled a laugh out of Pierre.

The unusual sound bounced off the walls of his room. He needed to put up some artwork or get a rug or two—at least fill the space. Minimalism was fine, but the room contained only the bed and a chest of drawers. "But does it matter, Lisette, when it's only you and I to see it?"

Lisette took the opportunity to leap onto him, hooking her claws into the cotton twill of his trousers. The neighbor boy would be coming over daily to feed and play with her, but she seemed to know he was going away.

"*Non!*" He extracted the kitten by the scruff, then cuddled her in the crook of his arm, stroking her pale belly. Lisette relaxed abruptly in the way of the young, purring extravagantly, all four white paws in the air as he petted her soft fur. "You can tell I'm leaving, can't you?"

Grief surged over him in a wave.

Pierre hadn't always been alone with only a cat for company and a bare apartment. Once, he'd had a busy life filled with friends and a beautiful, colorful home decorated by his artistically talented wife, and best of all, a little girl named Lucie who yelled, "Papa, don't go!" as she'd wrap her arms around his legs.

Pierre closed his eyes. Bittersweet agony rolled through him, and his breath hitched painfully. A tear hit Lisette's belly. The kitten opened her yellow eyes, startled, and batted at his hand. He set her down, and she scampered off.

Pierre dashed the moisture off his face; it had been a while since he'd shed an actual tear. Almost seven years after Gita and Lucie's deaths, he now welcomed these moments. They would always deserve his tears, whenever they came.

He continued his packing, but paused as his phone, lying beside the bag, chimed with an incoming message from Connor.

He sat down on the bed and picked up the device. Travel information filled the screen: the time and location of the private jet he'd be taking to the island of Bali's capital city, Denpasar. *"You'll be working with the same two operatives as last time; they will meet you at the airport and take you to the Yām Khûmkạn safe house there. A computer setup awaits; information regarding the assignment will be sent you via encrypted e-mail. Please confirm."*

"Copy that," Pierre texted back. *"Will check in when I arrive."*

He waited a couple of beats, but no further communication came through.

The Master of the Yām Khûmkạn was no longer making any effort to be friendly, and why should he? Pierre got to see the man's girlfriend and her children daily; he was a rival for their affections, if nothing more.

Yes, Pierre had lost everything and everyone who mattered years ago, but he had a new family to enjoy for as long as that lasted. He was grateful for that, even if his hopes for a romance with Sophie had been dashed.

His phone chimed again; this time it was Hermoine Leede, the petite forensic accountant he had struck up a friendship with on one of his previous cases. *"Got dinner plans? I just found the best little Asian fusion restaurant I've been wanting to try. Was hoping for company."*

Why not? He'd told Sophie he was going out with Heri Leede. Might as well give that some truth. *"Excellent. Where and when?"*

It would be good to get out of the empty apartment, and as Heri liked to say in her crisp British accent, "A body's got to eat."

🌴

Heri Leede was a woman of many talents; one of them was changing her appearance to project a different look whenever she chose to. Raveaux had seen Heri dress as if she wasn't a day under sixty—and other times, even with naturally white hair, she looked no older than he was.

Tonight, in a pair of skinny black jeans and a fuchsia pink cotton twin set, the four-foot eleven former Scotland Yard investigator appeared even younger. Her smile was wide as she reached up for a hug. "Pierre! It's been too long."

"Agreed." He held Heri by the shoulders, enjoying the way her bright blue eyes sparkled at him from behind rhinestone edged eyeglasses. "You're adorable."

"Why, thank you," Heri beamed. "And you're as tasty as a crumpet at teatime, per usual. Let's get caught up." She slid an arm through his and tugged him toward the tasteful entrance of the restaurant. "What have you been up to?"

"The usual, plus a bit of international travel." Pierre pushed open the door and led her inside. "Recently got back from abroad, and about to fly to Indonesia."

"Oh! How lovely! You must tell me all about it."

Soon they were seated in a booth lit by a sculptural paper lantern mounted on the wall and a small, softly glowing orb on the shiny onyx table. They ordered after a few minutes of chit-chat, and the waitstaff brought them warm cups of miso soup and a pot of green tea to begin their meal. Raveaux was suddenly famished.

Heri reached across the table to grasp his hands in her tiny, beringed ones. "What takes you to Indonesia?"

"A case. Can't discuss it, but I can tell you about my trip to Paris." Raveaux regaled her with the story of how he'd played the part of an art assessor at a major art event, authenticating a Cassat painting at auction before an audience of well-heeled onlookers. "One of my best performances. It helps that I'd had to check over so many forgeries in the past. How about you? What have you been working on since I saw you last?"

"Oh, nothing nearly so fun. You saw what I do on that case we worked on together. Spreadsheets. So many spreadsheets!" She gave an eye roll. "I recently tracked some major money laundering activity being hidden by a nonprofit that purported to save the whales. Talk about irony."

Raveaux listened to Heri's anecdote, a smile tugging at his mouth. If only he could feel something more for this smart, hilarious, attractive woman . . . Maybe he just needed to spend more time with Heri, give the relationship a chance.

"Let's get together more when I'm back from this trip," he said abruptly.

Heri cocked her head like a curious bird, her pale hair gilded by the low light. "Are we dating, then?"

His neck heated with embarrassment. "I'd like to spend time with you—see what happens. Do we need to define that right now?"

Heri smiled in that way she had, as if her whole face and body lit up. "I always push too hard for answers. Hazard of the profession! I'd like to spend more time with you too. Let's start there."

Mercifully, their food arrived, and the awkward moment passed.

Pierre walked Heri to the door of her townhouse after giving her a ride home in his Peugeot. Her place was in a gated community outside of the downtown area, conveniently close to the metro heart of Honolulu but far enough away for the pleasant cul-de-sac of adjoining units to feel private and quiet, surrounded as it was by a high, sound-deadening security wall hidden in tropical vines.

Glancing around, he saw Heri's personality in hand-painted stones in bright colors that lined a walkway lit by small solar lanterns. An antique carousel horse beside her front door held a brass mailbox; pots of geraniums softened the stairs. "Lovely home you have."

"Isn't it, though?" Heri gave a shy smile. "Want to come in for a nightcap?"

He shook his head regretfully. "Early flight tomorrow."

Heri took the rejection well, reaching up to give him a peck on the cheek. "Good night then, and bon voyage."

It was her graciousness that undid him. Pierre took Heri in his arms and drew her close; she fit well against him, her body petite and firm. He kissed her, and her lips tasted of the orange after-dinner liqueur they'd shared, and of loneliness, too; it was a good kiss that lasted a bit.

He set Heri back, gave her a hug, and waited for her to unlock her door—and felt a bit sad that he had no desire for anything more.

8

Day 4

The next morning, Sophie turned her SUV into the imposing entrance of Kama'aina Schools on her way to meet Dr. Ka'ula's security staffer in charge of student social media monitoring.

A winding driveway edged by *hapu'u* fern trees took her past a perfectly groomed track and field area. She navigated a broad turnaround in front of the imposing main administrative building; the roundabout circled a beautiful bronze fountain featuring a sculpture of a Hawaiian family harvesting taro.

Sophie exited the roundabout and passed beyond the instructional buildings, studying the campus with its well-maintained rolling lawns. High at the top of the enormous parklike area was the core administrative building, where Sophie turned in.

She had been to this site before, on another case involving embezzlement from the prestigious school's trust. Founded by the last of Hawaiian royalty, the school was mainly funded by the lease of expensive lands once owned by the crown, and paid for by the many high-rises of downtown Waikiki.

Sophie exited the vehicle, grabbing her backpack that doubled as a briefcase. "*Excrement of a flatulent yak!*" Sean had spit up on the item just before she left the house. She reached into the back seat and grabbed for a baby wipe handily positioned between the car seats. She scrubbed at the tough fabric. "You'd think I could get out of the house without being covered in spit-up at least once."

"I was just giving up on you," a voice spoke from Sophie's elbow. Old reflexes brought Sophie flying around to drop into a fighting stance, facing whoever addressed her.

The speaker was a medium-sized female with spiky dark hair tipped with bright blue streaks. Light brown skin, wide cheekbones and full lips spoke of mixed-race heritage. The woman took a step back as she faced Sophie's fierce gaze. "Sorry for startling you. I have a talent for sneaking up on people."

"No, it's I who should apologize. I'm late, and I overreacted. You must be Char Leong." Sophie stepped back too, slamming the car door and hefting her backpack onto a shoulder.

"Yes, I'm Char. Short for Charlotte." Leong had straight white teeth and a pair of deep dimples when she smiled. "Your assistant, Lono Jones, set up a meeting for us to talk about the security and social media accounts here at the school."

"Jones would not enjoy being called my assistant," Sophie said. "He's my partner at Security Solutions. An ex-Maui Police Department Detective."

The woman's almond-shaped eyes crinkled. "Oh yeah? I am a former HPD police officer. After five years on the force, I took this job because it's more family-friendly. I recognize a fellow mom when I see one." She pointed to the wipe in Sophie's hand, and the pair of car seats that filled the back seat of the SUV.

"Guilty as charged. I was once an FBI agent and an MMA fighter, if you can believe it. Now I'm a part-time CEO and investigator, and the full-time mother of two." Sophie gestured to the backpack. "I cannot seem to get out of the house on time or unscathed by baby effluents."

"Baby effluents! That's a new phrase. Our Willy is two, and the hubby and I are talking about having another one. But shoots, this job has been more challenging than I thought. It's got moments I never had to deal with as a police officer. This whole investigation is one of them." Leong cocked her head towards the entrance of the building. "Let's go up to my office."

Sophie nodded. She trailed Leong into the building and up a flight of stairs, noticing that the woman's well-defined back and muscular shoulders filled the tight polo shirt she wore in the school's trademark colors. "Do you work out, Char?"

"I do, as a matter of fact. Fitness is my outlet. I pretty much don't have anything else going on in my life besides work and family."

"I can relate." Sophie liked Leong's ready openness and upbeat energy.

Could she have discovered a possible new friend? Lei was so busy with career and family on Maui, and Marcella, not yet a mom and caught up in her work, was hardly ever available. Finding women Sophie connected with since the babies were born had been next to impossible.

Leong's office was a cramped cubicle off the main employee lounge. Cluttered with file boxes and office supplies, the desk obscured by three computer monitors, there was nowhere for Sophie to sit. Leong appeared unfazed by this; she moved a pile of file boxes off a folding chair, picked it up, and opened it behind her desk. "Squeeze in back here. Be easiest if we log in together, and I explain what I've been up to with this strategy."

Sophie slid off her backpack and maneuvered around the boxes to sit beside Leong as the security operative sat down in front of her cockpit of computers.

"First of all, let me punt you all my passwords and logins," Leong said, her fingers flying on an ergonomic keyboard that Sophie approved of. "I've already prepared a list of the sites I've used to monitor student activity for you, with their passwords."

"I looked at some of them." Sophie leaned in to see a half dozen app windows pop open on Leong's screens. "That's when I knew I needed to meet with you. I couldn't understand what I was seeing. These kids seem to speak their own language."

Leong snorted a laugh. "You got that right. When I was hired,

Dr. Ka'ula asked me to make monitoring school gossip and cyberbullying the focus of my job. Our staffers each have an area of focus on campus; I consider mine one of the most important, as cyberbullying is a source of many concerns at the school." Leong glanced at Sophie; her expression somber. "It has certainly been an education. But you'll like my avatar." She swiveled one of the monitors so Sophie could see a pixyish animation with blue antennae and a pair of bright blue wings. "My screen name is SoBee. I am sixteen, love mangoes, shave ice, several bands whose name I won't bore you with, and I am good at animation drawings. No boyfriend, but I've got crushes on the usual popular guys."

Sophie smiled. "Your avatar looks fun and likeable. I'd tell you my gossip."

"That's the idea." Leong oriented Sophie to her different identities and the tone of her interactions. "Now, how do you want to proceed with this?"

"First, show me anything and everything you have on the Moli Massacre," Sophie said. "And the sale of live eggs. Turns out there's been a theft of those on Maui, and we're worried that something that started here is spreading to that island too."

"Oh no! I passed what I had on to the headmaster; it wasn't much, but it was enough to make us realize that our students were involved in that terrible crime."

Leong showed Sophie the picture of the egg that she had already seen, and a file of screenshots that showed interactions alluding to the attack from two seemingly male identities. "The trouble is that we can't actually tell who these students are," Leong said. "And the posts were made from phones, so we can't track an IP address."

"I have a tracking device called a Stingray. If we get an indicative post in real time, you can use it to locate the phone by its embedded identity number," Sophie said. "The Stingray will pick up the signal and show its location and potential owner."

Leong nodded. "Great. Those things are expensive and supposed to be law enforcement only, or I'd already have one."

"Security Solutions has several." Sophie smiled at the other woman. "We have our ways. I'll have a device messengered over to you after we meet." She leaned in to point at one of the apps, a social site that featured time-limited posts that disintegrated after viewing. Viewers were by invitation only. "How did you build a connection with these kids so that they invited you to see their posts?"

Leong slanted Sophie a look. "Did you see my avatar? My alter ego is uber-cool. Everyone wants to know who she is—and nobody does. It's the spice of the unknown, plus popularity."

Sophie's years at a Geneva boarding school had not been pleasant; she had been both the wrong color and too introverted and tech-oriented to make friends with other girls, and her height and physical prowess had been off-putting to the boys. She'd spent most of high school ensconced in the library, gym, or in her room, alone.

Sophie shook her head regretfully. "I don't think I can replicate your presence online. Maybe I should passively mirror your interactions on my computer. If I have something I want to put out there, I'll let you know." Sophie continued as Leong leaned away from the monitors, swiveling to face her. "I want to find out more about the live eggs. Where they might be going, and of course who is selling them. Discovering who is buying them might help us track back to the source. How can we devise a social media post to lure out more information on that subject?"

Leong tapped a finger on her chin as she gazed up and to the left, considering. Her nails were short and unvarnished; Sophie approved. "There's a Fabergé egg inspired art contest being planned by the art and history departments. World history class has been studying the period of the Romanovs, and they and the art staff decided to coordinate their efforts to create a little more interest in that time period. Maybe I can come up with something fishing around for an idea, drawing an egg with a Laysan Albatross chick in it? Put my idea out there and see if someone gets eager to share—or brag."

"I like it. I could not come up with this angle to create an inquiry on my own."

Leong smiled. "Glad we'll be working together on this, then. Let's exchange numbers. You can text me, and I can do the same when I've got something I want you to see."

Sophie input Leong's personal cell number, and they exchanged a quick hello on their devices to make sure their numbers were saved.

"Now. My avatar is very arty. What kind of project would she want to come up with? This is the fun part for me." Leong pulled up another app; this one was a drawing program. Within a few moments she had imported several Fabergé egg images from the internet. She began a playful animation, and inside one of them, she inserted a fuzzy gray download of a *moli* chick.

"I can't believe how fast you came up with that art." Sophie was amazed. "You're really good at this!"

"Well, I'm hoping to have time for my art when the kids are older. Notice I'm saying 'the kids' as if we already have a complete family, and we're just beginning. But a girl's gotta dream." Leong typed rapidly, finishing her content upload.

The post at the bottom read, *"Where can I get a real, original photo of a moli chick escaping the egg? Would be a fun way to win the art contest!"* She threw a couple of animated emojis around the corner of the art piece, then turned the monitor to Sophie. "Too obvious?"

"Maybe it is. Why don't you just suggest a chick, but include the picture of the moli?"

Leong turned back, her fingers flying as she made a few corrections. She then posted the art piece on several of her social media sites under her avatar. "Now to let this percolate."

"Meanwhile, I can track that art online with my software," Sophie said. "I have a program that does data mining for keywords and images. We can look for more pictures and posts featuring the word albatross, Laysan, *moli*, and so forth."

"Sounds good. Anything else you think we can get going right now?"

"Not sure." Sophie rubbed the scar on her cheekbone absently as she considered Leong. "I wanted to contact you, dig into your social media situation and see how you handled it, and come up with some sort of plan to phish around. We've done that. Too bad." Sophie smiled. "I was having fun."

Leong grinned. "Me too. Have you tried the food here? We have a good staff lunch."

Sophie stomach gave a loud gurgle in reply. "I barely got out of the house properly dressed, let alone fed for the day."

Leong laughed. "Let's get something to eat and get to know each other a little better."

Sophie followed Char Leong to the door, feeling the best lift in her mood that she'd had in days. She had been actively fighting the black wings of encroaching depression lately. Triggers abounded: she was hiding in a house she'd made into a fortress with her family, hoping to defend her children from her murderous mother even as that primary betrayal ate at her soul.

She and Connor were a couple now, but with the threat of Pim Wat curtailing their lives, seeing each other occasionally was the best they could dream of for the indefinite future. Would they even be able to keep their relationship alive long-distance?

She also nursed nagging worries about her father.

Ambassador Frank Smithson had been dodging her calls, and she couldn't help remembering how reduced in health he'd seemed the last time she saw him.

"Ground yourself in the current moment," her friend and therapist Dr. Wilson said in her mind. "Notice what your senses are telling you. Let them pull you into the *now*. And usually, the 'now' is not so bad."

Sophie grounded herself in the 'now.'

She had discovered a potential friend in Char Leong, and she was entering a pleasantly decorated staff lounge with the possibility of good food soon.

A counter along one wall held a coffeemaker and condiments, a water dispenser, and a sink. Couches covered in the school's blue brand color made an inviting L in one corner. A long dining table decorated with boxes of treats and flowers was surrounded by chatting staffers eating a delicious-looking salad and beef stir-fry over rice that filled the air with mouthwatering smells.

"We just pick up the phone and order lunch. A student will bring our plates," Leong said. "You have a choice of vegetarian or beef."

"I'll take the beef." Sophie patted her belly. "Need maximum protein."

Leong nodded and reached for the phone. "I'll place our order with the kitchen."

A moment later, as Leong set the phone down after ordering, the door to the lounge opened. The headmaster, Dr. Ka'ula, entered, followed by a short, sturdy woman dressed in the school's staff uniform of royal blue polo shirt and black pants.

Ka'ula started visibly at the sight of Sophie and Leong, then regrouped. "Just the women I need to see. I have an urgent situation. Come with me."

9

Sophie once again followed Char Leong upstairs and down a hallway —but this time they were trailing headmaster Ka'ula and the woman he'd brought with him, not yet introduced.

Dr. Ka'ula pushed open a door at the end of the hall and made a "please enter" gesture. "This is our staff conference room. The students will bring your lunches up here and we can have more privacy."

Sophie looked around; the room was utilitarian, with a laminate Formica conference room table lined with plastic chairs, whiteboards on the walls, and a podium. Hawaiian and US flags hung limply from stands in the corners. Sophie easily visualized the announcements and seminars for teachers that took place in the room.

Ka'ula drew out a chair at the head of the table. The women took seats on either side of him.

Sophie studied the staffer in the blue polo shirt with interest. She was built like a fireplug, strong and square through the hips and shoulders; dark brown deep-set eyes, almost hidden in folds of tawny skin, stared back at Sophie. Her hair was parted severely in the middle, and that strip of bare scalp had been tattooed with geometric symbols. Two long plaits hung down over her shoulders.

Clearly, Leong and the counselor knew each other; they exchanged nods.

Ka'ula introduced the woman to Sophie at last. "This is Dharma Dawnhorse. She's one of our school counselors and specifically assigned to the eleventh grade. We have two counselors per grade; one of them handles student needs, and the other focuses on college prep and applications. Ms. Dawnhorse is our student needs counselor."

"Sophie Smithson with Security Solutions." Sophie gave Dawnhorse a smile. "Pleased to meet you."

"Hello." Ms. Dawnhorse had a low, melodious voice. "Welcome to Kama'aina Schools."

"Ms. Smithson was reviewing the social media accounts with me." Char Leong addressed Dr. Ka'ula. "We will be partnering on monitoring them for activity regarding the investigation that brings Ms. Smithson here."

"Fine, fine." Ka'ula seemed stressed; tiny beads of sweat had gathered along his dense black hairline. "I thought this meeting was fortuitous, because Ms. Smithson is investigating the Moli Massacre." He addressed this to Dawnhorse, then turned to Sophie and Leong who sat on his other side. "This is a delicate situation because of student confidentiality, but Ms. Dawnhorse came to me with a concern about a student who has verbalized suicidal thoughts—and the source might be his involvement in the crime."

Sophie's eyes widened in surprise, and Dawnhorse inclined her head in a dignified way. "Normally I wouldn't reach out to administration, but with the danger to the student, I decided I had to break the child's confidentiality." She reached into a large, hand-tooled leather purse that hung from her shoulder and produced a drawing. She placed the paper on the table and then slid it over to Sophie. "The student in question comes in weekly for counseling for depression since becoming a target of ongoing bullying. He often talks about his dreams or shares art about them. He claims this art is from a dream."

The drawing was done in oil pastel, and the style was expressionistic; a scarlet background set off wheeling shapes of white birds with long, black-tipped wings. Crude slash marks on the birds bled into the red background.

Repellently violent, the drawing made Sophie want to look away. "You said this boy was having suicidal thoughts?"

"Yes. He's had those before, but this was worse. He described having access to a weapon and a desire to follow through. I notified his mother, and she picked him up from school to go to a private therapist for further evaluation and possible inpatient treatment."

Sophie met the woman's stern gaze. "Seems like you did the right thing to make sure your student was safe."

Dawnhorse's eyes softened. "The children are always my top priority."

"Tell me more about the bullying this student has been experiencing."

"The student won't give me names, but he has said the main bully is a high-status male student who has been taking his money and making him perform tasks to prove his worthiness of being a friend."

"Could one of those tasks have been attacking the birds? Stealing their eggs?" Sophie asked.

A short nod from Dawnhorse. "Other than the art, though, he has not said anything directly."

"We need the student's name," Dr. Ka'ula rapped out.

"I cannot give that to you. Under the Tarasoff precedent, I must break the boy's confidentiality to prevent harm to the student by himself, or to others by him, i.e., a suicidal or homicidal threat I deem to be actionable. I have done so by notifying his parent; hopefully he is safe now. An indirect confession to a crime, such as this piece of art—while related to his state of mind—is not something I can break confidentiality about," Dawnhorse said in her dignified way.

Ka'ula's neck reddened with temper. "This will be going in your employee file, Ms. Dawnhorse."

Dawnhorse folded her lips tightly, her expression an indifferent mask, though she lifted her chin proudly.

Char Leong moved restlessly, clearly uncomfortable with witnessing her colleague's dressing down. "Dharma has to do what she thinks is right professionally, Dr. Ka'ula."

An attempt to de-escalate the situation was in order. Sophie leaned toward the counselor. "I respect your parameters, Ms. Dawnhorse. I'm a professional too; I specialize in technical and online investigation. Is there any other information you can give me that might help shed light on this student and his plight?"

The four of them sat tensely as Dawnhorse thought this over. "The student does do a lot of art," she said at last. "He may have planned to enter the Fabergé-inspired contest the history and art departments are organizing."

"Thank you," Sophie said. "I recognize that you're sharing a confidential bit of information because this piece of art is part of his record with you. However, Ms. Leong and I may be able to tease out who it is from knowing that he's entering the contest." She steepled her fingers. "Ultimately, we want to find who is behind the attacks, the ringleader as it were, and stop that person from bullying others, including your student. You're doing the right thing in helping us get there."

Dawnhorse gave a short nod. "I have appointments to keep, if that's all?" She addressed the wall above Ka'ula's head.

"You're dismissed." The headmaster's tone indicated his ongoing displeasure.

Dharma Dawnhorse got up and left, taking the piece of student art with her—but Sophie'd had a chance to snap a quick picture of it with her phone. She caught Char Leong's eye and a silent communication passed between the two women as Sophie tapped her phone and sent Leong the photo.

Leong cleared her throat. "I believe our lunch has gone missing, Dr. Ka'ula. If that's all?"

"Go find your meal and you can meet Ms. Smithson in the lounge when I'm done speaking with her privately," Ka'ula said.

Leong exited. The door closed gently behind her, leaving the two of them alone.

Sophie turned in her chair to face the headmaster. "Dr. Ka'ula, this meeting was, indeed, fortuitous. I'm confident that Ms. Leong and I will be able to figure out the lead Ms. Dawnhorse gave us regarding her client entering the art contest. We were already developing an angle to phish for the perps using that contest." She met the headmaster's gaze directly. "Please don't sanction your counselor for upholding her professional standards."

Ka'ula set his jaw. "It sets a bad precedent for Dawnhorse to defy a direct request from administration."

"Speaking as someone who is the CEO of a major company, I politely disagree." Sophie maintained eye contact with the belligerent headmaster, though it was uncomfortable; her history of abuse had conditioned her to withdraw in such situations. "Enabling your employees to uphold the standards and criteria of their professions is important for the long-term success of the school. If you profess to want to end bullying on campus, you must model that from the top."

Ka'ula's eyes widened; he glanced away and took a breath, then sighed it out, sagging visibly. "I didn't realize I was doing that." He covered his face with his hands.

"The mark of a good leader is the ability to make mistakes, own them, and learn from them," Sophie said gently. "Sometimes, apologies are also necessary."

"I'll speak to Dawnhorse," Ka'ula said, lowering his hands. He stared at his broad palms as if they might hold answers. "Enjoy your lunch with Leong and keep me posted on progress. Thanks for protecting *my* confidentiality as your client."

"Of course." Sophie rose. She rested a hand briefly on Ka'ula's beefy shoulder. "And thank you for being willing to go the extra mile to solve this case. You didn't have to hire us, and that you did so speaks well of your character. This is not an easy situation."

She left the headmaster alone with his thoughts and headed for the teacher's lounge.

Char Leong was seated at the now deserted staff dining table, picking at a metal tray loaded with the food Sophie had glimpsed earlier. Another tray, covered with foil, rested at her elbow.

Sophie glanced around the room. "Can we speak privately here?"

Leong glanced at the clock. "Yeah. Afternoon classes just began; we shouldn't run into any more teachers."

Sophie slid into a chair opposite Leong. She pulled the aluminum tray over and uncovered a generous portion of beef stir-fry over a mound of rice, and a pile of crispy salad. "Looks good."

The women ate quietly for several minutes.

Finally, Sophie set her fork aside and popped open the small carton of milk that had accompanied her meal. She took a generous swig. "Even though I'm feeding a baby, I forget how nutritious milk can be. Got another of these?"

Leong indicated a large silver refrigerator on one wall. "Help yourself."

Sophie fetched another carton of milk and returned to dig into the remainder of the meal. When she'd finished, she dabbed her mouth with a napkin. "Mm. I was hungry."

Leong had only stirred her food around; most of it remained. "I've got a bit of a stomachache after that meeting."

"I should have told you right away—Ka'ula has reconsidered his position on writing up Dawnhorse."

Leong's eyes widened. "Really?"

"I pointed out that curbing bullying begins at the top." Sophie finished the last of her second carton of milk.

"Only a non-employee could get away with something like that with him," Leong said a bit sourly. She picked up her fork and began eating.

"Ka'ula's stubborn, but he has a good heart and wants to do the right thing, from what I can tell," Sophie said. Too bad she couldn't inform Leong that the headmaster was the one who'd hired Security Solutions! "Anyway. I wanted to touch base about our game plan for finding this student and make sure you received the photo I sent you of his art." She cocked her head. "I thought maybe you could review the art contest submissions for something that looks like a similar style, if the phishing plan doesn't lure him out first."

"Excellent. I did get the photo. I'll contact the art teacher in charge of submissions. Should be no problem; she's a friend and a bird lover. She'll be happy to help us screen for art that might hint at involvement in the Moli Massacre." Leong cleaned her plate and then picked up Sophie's, too. She carried the trays to a trolley and sorted the items into different areas for washing. "I'd like to get started on that right away."

"Perfect." Sophie stood. "Is there anything else I can help with right now?"

"I don't think so." Leong returned to face Sophie. "Let me just review the plan and make sure I haven't missed anything." She held up a hand and ticked off items on her fingers. "One: I'll monitor that post about my contest submission and see if any students chime in with useful leads. Two: you'll send over one of those Stingrays for me to use on campus and try to catch the student's phone that leads might be coming from. Three: I'll check the art department submissions for the Fabergé contest and look for a match to this student art."

"And four: you'll text me the minute anything comes through to you of interest, and five: I'll be monitoring your social media accounts with my own data mining software," Sophie said.

"And six: we'll meet up sometime soon to work out together," Leong said, playfully flexing an arm.

Sophie gave Leong a fist bump. "I really like that last one."

🌴

Sophie's mood was much improved from the morning as she drove toward home. Not only did she and Leong have a plan for the case, but she might even have found a friend.

As if that thought had conjured it, her phone rang with a call from Lei on Maui. She took the call, routed through the car's audio system. "Good morning, Lei."

"Hey, lady, it's afternoon." Lei chuckled. "You still in the new mom haze?"

"I did lose track of time. I'm working on the case. Been following up with some leads that indicate that teens may be involved," Sophie said.

Lei's voice sobered immediately. "Can you come over to Maui and meet the organizers of the Albatross Sanctuary in Waihee? I could really use some backup. My lieutenant has told me I can't work the case when I've got homicides to solve, but my gut is telling me yours and mine are related. It's urgent and time-sensitive if we have a chance to rescue live eggs."

Sophie tapped her fingers on the steering wheel as she navigated the downtown Waikiki traffic. "A trip to Maui wouldn't be a part of the investigation here and wouldn't be billable to our client, so I'd be doing it pro bono. I also need to confer with Armita regarding childcare—but maybe I could bring Sean since I'm breastfeeding and he's not mobile yet."

"I get it." Lei blew out a breath. "It's a lot to ask. But it would be a treat to have you come stay overnight with us; Kiet would love to see Auntie Sophie and I'm dying to get a look at that baby." She paused. "I'm basically investigating this thing off the books too. The *moli* have found their way into my heart."

"Well, then, we should do it," Sophie said. "If Armita's agreeable to me being gone overnight, I'll come over. I'll text you as soon as I know."

"Thanks so much."

"And maybe by then I'll know something more. We've got several lures in the water, as the fishermen say."

"Good. I'll wait to hear from you, then, and set up a tentative meet with the conservation group," Lei said. "Talk soon, *sistah*!"

10

Day 4

Raveaux sat in the small, luxuriously appointed private lounge that was a part of the private air flight area of Honolulu International Airport. The Security Solutions company jet was already fueled, provisioned, and the crew were on board, but Raveaux still awaited the arrival of the two Thai operatives from the Yām Khûmkạn—Sam and Rab, that he had worked with when last pursuing Pim Wat.

Raveaux sat back in a leather recliner with a moveable work desk pulled across his lap. Opening his laptop, he reviewed the information Connor had forwarded, little as it was: a petite female of Pim Wat's size and build had been spotted leaving the crime scene where a prominent Balinese businessman suspected of having ties to drug smuggling had been murdered. The information had come to Raveaux in an encrypted file, a series of news clippings translated from law enforcement communiques, and one very generic news item.

The only pictures included were the police photos of the crime scene, which told him that the man had been executed with three small caliber shots: one to the head, two to the heart. Clearly a pro had done it, but was the assassin Pim Wat?

"It's not enough," Pierre muttered aloud.

This lead was too little information for which to go all the way to Bali with any real hope of a break in the hunt. The victim was Balinese, which meant local authorities would be all over it. Raveaux and the ninjas, as outsiders, would stand out: none of them knew the language, customs, nor did they have any contacts on Bali besides the CIA.

They were bound to draw attention in a negative way by poking around.

If the assassin was Pim Wat, she would have done the job and left —unless Bali was her new base of operations, which it might be. But in that case, she'd be a fool to draw heat in her new hometown, and Pim Wat was no fool.

No.

Raveaux wasn't going to go to Bali.

He'd take his crew and the jet to a place where he knew the rules, both written and unwritten—where he spoke the language and was a native with the advantage of connections and familiarity. He'd go where Pim Wat's boss, Enrique Mendoza, lived.

Paris.

Raveaux wasn't Connor's lackey to be ordered around the globe on a whim. He was an experienced investigator who knew how to get results. After all, he'd been the one to solve the mystery of Pim Wat's disappearance the last time that slippery witch made her escape.

Connor would thank him later when the job was done.

Raveaux closed the laptop decisively, flipped up the foldable desk, and got up from the lounger. He slid the computer into his familiar leather satchel, tucked his latest Reacher novel into the capacious pocket of his jacket, and headed out through the glare-resistant glass doors onto the tarmac. He was on his way to redirect the Security Solutions pilot to a new destination.

Sam and Rab, ninjas with the Yām Khûmkạn, greeted Raveaux an hour later at the base of the movable stairs leading up to the jet's entrance.

"Bonjour, Pier." Rab greeted Pierre with the shorthand name they'd come up with the last time the three men met. Sam, who only spoke Thai, nodded.

"Bonjour, Rab, Sam. Come on up, and I'll bring you up to speed."

"Speed?" Rab cocked his head.

"Sorry—meaning that I'll brief you on a change of plans."

Rab nodded and translated for Sam. The two followed as Raveaux ascended the steps onto the jet. Each carried a duffel and a heavy-looking metal case; these were likely chock-full of weapons—a good reason to fly private.

Both Thai men wore their usual head-to-toe black, but their clothing was appropriate for the new destination—pants and long-sleeved shirts, rather than the martial arts outfits they normally favored. Raveaux took a seat and waited until Rab and Sam had stowed their gear in the storage areas.

The Learjet was equipped with comfortable, reclinable leather seats facing each other across from a stationary coffee table. Rab sat across from Raveaux, settling himself. Light streaming in through the jet's round porthole highlighted silver in the stubble of his closely shorn head, but only that and a few crinkles beside intelligent dark eyes betrayed the fact that Rab was older than his partner. Both men carried themselves with an air of calm confidence.

The co-pilot stuck his head out from the cabin. "We're cleared for the new flight plan. Taking off in five."

"*Merci*," Raveaux said, engaging his seatbelt. He leaned forward to address the two operatives. "Remember the man you tracked who directs Pim Wat? We will be capturing him and extracting her location from him. We're going to Paris instead of Bali."

Rab's eyes brightened with a feral gleam; he'd been the one to propose that they snatch Mendoza and interrogate him for Pim Wat's location before she'd slipped away the last time. "This is good plan." He turned and translated rapidly to Sam, who nodded in comprehension and agreement.

"While we're in flight, I want you two to figure out a plan to take Mendoza without alerting any of his associates or the authorities. You know his routine, his home and business locations already. If there's anything specific you need for your plan, let me know. Meanwhile, I'm going to be working on a location where we can take him to get the information we need."

Rab nodded. "This is a good strategy," he said in his careful English. "We will do. We will need a map of Paris to begin."

"I'm sure that can be easily obtained."

The plane taxied out of its parking slot. Raveaux sat back, relaxing in the headrest's soft leather cradle. He watched the highrises, palm trees, and vivid, sharply cut green peaks of Oahu's Koʻolau Mountains speed by as they took off—and when the jet heeled over in a turn, he enjoyed the turquoise and indigo ocean, dotted with watercraft and the shadows of reefs, receding below.

He hadn't said goodbye to Sophie. Would she even notice? Raveaux rubbed the left side of his chest. It always seemed to ache when he thought of her.

At least her daughter Momi would miss him. "Unco Perro" was gone, and she'd ask for him. Pierre would enjoy finding his goddaughter a gift in Paris.

A small thing to look forward to, but it was enough. He fell asleep.

11

Connor sat down with the leaders of the different disciplines at the Yām Khûmkạn. He'd been having twice-daily meetings with them, using Robert's Rules of Order to run the meetings, and getting them used to casting a vote and letting the majority make decisions.

There was no shortage of issues to be solved: everything from a decline in recruitment and supply chain problems to plumbing and water purity challenges in the fortress's ancient structure. Some of the new recruits had even brought in phones and were insisting on staying connected with the outside world.

"Part of what makes our training effective is a complete disconnection from the outside," one of the team heads said. "We can't bend on this."

"Make a motion," Connor prompted, catching his eye. "Put it to a vote."

"Yes, Master." the man lowered his gaze. "As you say."

Connor rolled his eyes heavenward. "No, that's not what I meant. When someone decides there's been enough discussion on a topic, he can make a motion for a certain action to take place. If it's seconded, you can vote right away. Do you want to make a motion now?"

"I think we should discuss it more," the man said. "What do the rest of you think about the issue of phones for new recruits?"

The meeting progressed more smoothly after that. Connor sat back and folded his arms, watching proudly as eventually the team leader made the motion. It was seconded, and then everyone voted to have new recruits submit their phones and eventually earn them back as a reward, with limited use, at a certain level of achievement.

After the meeting, Connor joined the evening drill in the courtyard, going through the martial arts forms alongside the men.

Even as he stepped forward into the memorized sequence, punching, kicking, whirling in synchronized harmony with the others—his mind was elsewhere.

The conversation he'd had a few days earlier with McDonald still rankled. The CIA man was an ass and was using his power to humiliate Connor and keep him penned up in the Yām Khûmkạn fortress.

Connor hadn't even seen Sophie's new home yet. Now was the perfect time for him to sneak over to Oahu and visit Sophie and the kids. Pim Wat was somewhere far away; Raveaux would flush her out, but that wouldn't be for days. Meanwhile, Raveaux would be temporarily gone.

Connor could take the chopper to the airport and have the Security Solutions private jet fly in and pick him up in Bangkok. He'd adopt one of his aliases, complete with passport, and slip into Honolulu under the radar and—surprise her. He'd have to do it that way. Sophie would never agree to him visiting; the risk he'd be arrested was too great.

Once he'd made up his mind, energy flowed through Connor like electricity, and he flew through the exercises, tireless.

Feirn met him when the drill ended, as the men left the courtyard for dinner. Sunset played salmon pink rays over the lichen-covered, ancient stone walls. Oncoming night cooled the humid air: the birds sang their evening arias over the jungle. "I'd like to walk the ramparts," Connor said. "Come with me?"

"Of course, Master. Your meal will be kept hot until you're ready."

Connor nodded and took a close-by stair, heading for the highest level of the fortress. Cut into raw, unfinished rock, the steps were rough under his bare feet, but that didn't slow him. He took them two at a time until he stood on the flat parapet surrounding the topmost wall of the fortress.

Built in a style much different than a Western fortification, the cluster of buildings that made up the temple, training facility, and armed compound of the Yām Khûmkạn was a series of linked step pyramids within an encircling wall. The parapet Connor stood on was capped along the outer edge with jagged, unfinished rocks that had been cemented in; they formed a waist-high barrier that ended up leaving natural gaps useful for defense.

But no one, in all the centuries the fortress had stood, had attacked it; the jungle around it, and the men inside, were too formidable.

Connor gripped the coarse stone and gazed out over the jungle toward the horizon.

Night already deepened shadows beneath the dense canopy, but the birds were still awake. The chattering of a flock of mynah birds in their chosen sleeping tree came to him clearly, along with the shriek of a parrot, the croaking of frogs, and the occasional cry of an animal. The smell of onions and beans wafted from the vent that led to the men's dining area. Far off in the distance, the light pollution of Bangkok tinted the sky above the city with a faint orange hue.

Connor had been at the compound long enough that he was used to the sounds, smells, and sights of this forbidding place; it had even begun to feel comfortable. He'd never expected that. Even so, his eyes returned to the glow of light over a faraway city. His heart sped up with anticipation to leave and be with the woman he loved—no risk was too great.

"Connor?" Feirn's voice interrupted his reverie.

"Yes?"

"Is everything—all right?"

"Yes. But I'll be taking a trip soon. And only you will accompany me."

12

Day 5

Sophie slid into the front seat of her friend Lei's roomy Toyota Tacoma extended cab truck after the short flight to Maui the following day. Lei leaned over to give her a hug, her riot of brown curls tickling Sophie's nose.

"It's always so good to see you, girl! Did you forget something? Where's Sean?" Lei, her tilted brown eyes sparkling, looked around Sophie in an exaggerated way. "I wanted to kiss and smoosh some fat baby cheeks!"

"I talked it over with Armita, and we decided it was better to keep Sean on his schedule at home," Sophie said, smiling regretfully. "He's occasionally sleeping through the night now, and it's been so tough to get there that we didn't want to mess it up."

"Dang it, I really wanted to meet your little guy." Lei put the truck in gear and navigated away from the baggage claim area, merging into traffic as they passed streams of tourists crossing to the car rental kiosks. The wind Maui was famous for whipped the well-trimmed palm trees as Lei drove out of the airport. "I guess I'll have to come to Oahu."

"I'd love to show you my new house," Sophie said. "Kiet would enjoy the pool and the beach is right there, too."

"Okay, it's a deal. Meanwhile, I've set up a meeting with some reps from the Albatross Sanctuary out at the site tomorrow. We'll have dinner and an early bedtime tonight out at my place."

Sophie's stomach rumbled; she smiled and patted her abdomen. "My tummy agrees with that plan."

Sophie hadn't been able to visit Lei and her family at their compound in Haiku for a long time. Her spirits lifted as she and Lei drove along a familiar, narrow two-lane road through the jungle of East Maui. Red ti plants, mango and guava, and tall robusta eucalyptus decorated with ferns and dangling vines lined the route once they'd left scenic Hana Highway along the coast.

"Your commute is very pleasant," Sophie observed. "When do you think you might come to Oahu?"

"I don't know when we'll be able to make it, given the school schedule and with Stevens and I both working." Lei kept both hands on the wheel as she navigated a one-lane cement bridge. "But I'll sure look for an opportunity."

Soon they had reached the high wooden fence that marked the family's property, and Lei punched in the code at the gate. The barrier retracted, and Lei and Stevens's two Rottweilers bounded toward the truck, barking joyfully in their deep, booming voices.

Lei pulled the truck up and parked in the covered garage area of the simple, sturdy cement dwelling with its flame-retardant metal roof.

Kiet, a slender boy with unusual dark green eyes, appeared on the porch. "Mama!"

Ellen Stevens, Lei's husband's mom, followed the child as he descended a short flight of stairs toward them.

Sophie got out of the truck, swinging her backpack onto her shoulder. "Hello, Kiet. Remember me, Auntie Sophie? You've grown so tall since I saw you last!"

"Hi, Auntie. I'm five now." Kiet hugged Sophie around the midsection, and she patted his wiry back. Kiet was naturally shy, so his overture was heartwarming.

"Great to see you," Ellen said with a smile; the slender woman tucked pale blonde hair behind her ears. "It's been a while since you've come to Maui."

"Too long. I wish we all lived closer to each other," Sophie said. "How are you?"

"Very well, thanks. Blessed to be on the island to help take care of Kiet while his parents work. A grandma's dream come true."

"For us, too. Thanks, Ellen." Lei finished greeting the dogs and came around the truck, sweeping Kiet into her arms and smacking his cheeks with a kiss. "What's my little man been up to today?"

"Lots of reading!" Kiet chattered about his latest book and his day as Ellen waved goodbye and headed out to her little white Toyota Corolla.

The two women ascended the porch, the dogs pressing in behind Sophie as the three entered the house.

Lei, still carrying Kiet, headed for the kitchen. "I'll turn on the Instant Pot," she called over her shoulder. "I already prepped a big pork roast for kalua pig tonight."

"Doesn't that take hours?" Sophie glanced around the simple living room with its couch, coffee table, lounger and TV. A bookshelf filled one wall, jam-packed with books on the history, culture, animals, and plants of Hawaii, and the whole bottom row filled with well-worn children's stories. A striking painting of the rugged lance of the Iao Needle filled the wall beside the TV; Lei and her husband had lived in Iao Valley when they first moved to Maui years ago. "Your home is beautiful, Lei."

"It's nothing fancy, but it's fireproofed and big enough for all we need." Lei and Stevens had lost the original home on this property to fire a few years before.

Lei set Kiet on the counter where he could watch as she took out a large, wrapped roast and a lidded metal pot with a cord. "And to answer your question about how long the kalua pig takes, it'll be ready in an hour with this terrific invention." She patted the roundish metal device with its sturdy locking lid. "It's the new pressure cooker. A non-cook's best friend."

"This I've got to see," Sophie said. "Can you show me where I'll be sleeping and then demonstrate it for me?"

"Sure thing." Lei lifted Kiet down. "Show Auntie to her room, okay, little man?"

"Follow me, Auntie!" Kiet bellowed, and for just a moment he reminded Sophie of her uninhibited Momi as he ran down the hall, leading her to the bedroom at the far end, a tidy chamber that doubled as an in-home office and guest room.

Sophie followed her young guide, and then set her backpack beside the full-sized bed tucked in a corner. "Thanks, Kiet."

"Want to see my room?" Kiet cocked his head to look up at her through a lock of glossy black hair.

"Of course I do." Sophie brushed the forelock away so she could see Kiet's beautiful eyes. The little boy had been born in tragedy but had brought Lei and Stevens nothing but joy. Once again Sophie was grateful for her two babies, both of whom had been unplanned surprises. Though she would have no more thanks to medical intervention, she'd never regret Momi and Sean. They, too, brought joy and helped heal heartbreak.

The evening passed pleasantly as the family, joined by Lei's father Wayne who lived in the cottage next-door, enjoyed a simple, tasty meal of rice, kalua pig and steamed green beans. Sophie tried not to notice how many beers Lei's husband put away, though Stevens showed no signs of inebriation.

"Better get to bed," Lei told Sophie as they washed up and Stevens read a bedtime story to Kiet on the couch. "We've got a meeting with the Maui Albatross Sanctuary people out at the nesting site tomorrow morning, but I want to take you to breakfast for girl talk first."

"Sounds excellent." Sophie hugged her friend good night. "See you in the morning. I'm sure it will be a busy day." As she said it, an icy shiver of premonition tickled down her spine.

13

Day 6

Sophie eyed a delicious-looking plate of fried rice, papaya and eggs the next morning at Lei's favorite restaurant in Kahului, ready to take a bite, but her friend pinned her with a look. "So. What's going on with your love life?"

"Oh." Sophie set down the fork she'd picked up. She looked around the little hole-in-the-wall place that Lei favored. "I'm not sure I'm ready to talk about it."

"C'mon. Marcella told me you and the mysterious man in Thailand are back together. I want deets."

Sophie's neck prickled with embarrassment. "I know this is what women friends do, talk about their relationships . . . but—it's hard to explain." How could she put into words the connection she'd always felt with Connor, ever since their early cat and mouse games of online chase?

She'd loved Alika, and then Jake—but those relationships had been more physical, more visceral. What she had with Connor was nuanced, complicated, a meeting of minds and interests as much as bodies.

"It's okay." Lei's plate was filled with tempura and scrambled eggs. She picked up a shrimp and crunched it. "You don't have to get into it if you don't want to."

"I'm a little tired of people not supporting my choice to be with him, to be honest."

"Just because he's a cyber vigilante, an internationally wanted fugitive, and the cult leader of a shady ninja army?" Lei quirked a brow, a dimple appearing in her cheek.

"All of that is true." Sophie stirred at her eggs. Her appetite was gone. "But the worst parts would go away if we could catch my mother."

"Maybe." Lei dipped another shrimp into sauce. "To be honest, I don't care about any of that. I just want to know why you took him back after he—pretended to be dead and broke your heart. That would have been a deal breaker for me."

"He paid his debt for that mistake." Sophie gazed up at the dusty paper lantern above the table as she gathered her thoughts. "Connor joined the Yām Khûmkạn so that I could be with Jake. He got out of the way to support my choice. Through all the ups and downs with Jake, he continued to love me and show by his actions that he wanted what was best for me, not for himself necessarily. And then, he tried everything possible to save our lives when Jake and I were trapped by the volcano." Sophie picked up her cup and took a sip of green tea. "After he became the Master—for a while, he'd become someone I didn't know. He had evolved." She could not explain Connor's extraordinary abilities. "But when he was dying and I thought I'd lost him—I realized I'd always loved him in a way I never had anyone else, and that he was my match. My equal."

Lei's tilted brown eyes were intent on Sophie's. "Then I trust you've made the right choice," she said. "No one but those inside a relationship really know what's going on in it, anyway." Her mouth tightened.

Sophie took a bite of her breakfast. "How about you and Stevens?"

"We're going through a rough patch. He's got all the signs of PTSD, and he's drinking too much." Lei stabbed a piece of tempura with her fork. "But he's stubborn. I don't know how to help him. We're—in separate bedrooms."

"Oh no! Have you talked to Dr. Wilson?" Sophie and Lei had shared the police psychologist as a colleague and therapist over the years.

"Of course. She's working with him as much as he'll let her. But I worry—she's only getting a little bit of the truth." Lei shook her head. "If you'd asked me a few years ago if I thought we'd be in this kind of a jam, I'd have said you were crazy. But what happened with his first wife, Kiet's mother—it messed with his head on top of a buildup of ugly cases."

"Is there anything I can do?" Sophie reached across the table to touch Lei's hand. "I've been through violence as well."

"Yeah, you have. Maybe you could talk to him when we get home tonight? Encourage him to get real with Dr. Wilson, at least."

"I'll do that." Sophie wasn't confident that Lei's husband, who'd always been warm but impersonal toward her, would be open to any advice. "I'll certainly give it a try."

"Good." Lei waved for the check. "We just have time to get ourselves out to the Albatross Sanctuary for a look at the area before the board members arrive to meet with us."

The Maui Albatross Sanctuary was only thirty minutes away from downtown Kahului where the women had eaten breakfast. Sophie was glad she'd worn sturdy black athletic shoes and easy-movement pants as she trekked after Lei as her friend led her out of an unpaved dirt parking lot where they'd parked Lei's extended cab Toyota truck.

The two women hiked up a narrow dirt footpath between stunted *haole koa* trees bent in the direction of the prevailing wind toward a rise of land. Typical native plants grew among the short, shrubby trees, including the kind of *ipomoea* or beach morning glory vines that Sophie'd recently planted at her new home in Kailua.

Coconut palms rose from the brush here and there, along with gnarled, thorny *kiawe* trees. This area wasn't a lush jungle; whatever plant could thrive in dry and inhospitable conditions fought for life in the arid, reddish, sandy soil.

The two topped another small rise, and suddenly Sophie could see for miles in every direction: a wide-open stretch of dunes backed an empty coral sand beach bracketed by black, lava rock cliffs in one direction, and a bluff covered in ironwood trees the other.

Lei pointed to a tall chain-link fence a few hundred yards away. "That's the beginning of the albatross sanctuary area."

"The conditions at this site bear a resemblance to the nesting grounds at Ka'ena on Oahu," Sophie said. "Even the wind directionality is the same."

"The albatrosses ride in on the wind to land. They're so big they need to run in an open area and launch themselves off raised ground to get airborne when they take off," Lei said. "Doesn't surprise me that this mirrors the Oahu site."

As if to illustrate this, an albatross came soaring in on an updraft, tucked its wings, and dropped gracefully to the ground, where it trotted out of sight behind a clump of bushes.

"I can see how getting that much size off of the ground is a bit of challenge," Sophie said. "Those wings have to be six feet wide, at least."

"Yeah. I wanted you to get a look at the protected area before the members of the Albatross Sanctuary board meet us at the parking lot."

"I wish we had longer to explore. I'd love to walk around and see the nests."

"Me too. If only keeping the birds safe was as simple as fencing out the predators," Lei said. "For a long time, that's all people thought it would take—and that was hard enough to do with the land in danger of development, and the cost of building and monitoring that barrier."

The pair turned around, but not before Sophie had taken one last, long look at the stretch of rugged coast with its wide-open sea.

A distant plume of whale spout set off a row of flamboyant cumulus clouds that marched along the distant blue horizon.

"I never get tired of where I live." Lei's gaze was on the view.

"Nor do I." Sophie tightened Marcus's borrowed MPD ball cap so that it kept her curly ponytail from the wind's mischievous fingers. She smiled as she met Lei's eyes. "I love it here in Hawaii. I never want to be anywhere else."

Though she enjoyed the tiny Thai island of Phi Ni, it was too small and isolated for any great length of time; even Maui would be too quiet for her. Sophie relished the city life, and the many cultural and natural activities that busier Oahu offered.

Back at the parking lot, Lei introduced Sophie to three of the Albatross Sanctuary board members who'd arrived: Sari and Mahmoud Gadish, an older couple dressed in matching Columbia hiking wear, complete with hiking poles, and a tall, leathery-looking woman with a blunt gray bob named Dr. Danica Powers.

"Retired state biologist." Dr. Powers had a strong, dry grip that reminded Sophie of weightlifters she'd known. "Glad to have you here."

"I'm privately contracted to investigate the Moli Massacre on Oahu. This is strictly a volunteer side trip for me, since the cases might be related," Sophie said. "Tell me what each of your volunteer responsibilities are, please?"

"We're the financial backing," Mahmoud Gadish said. "We've paid for most of the fencing project. Maui is our home now that we've retired, and we want to help protect these magnificent birds."

"And our son, who is deceased, told us in a dream that he was returning to earth as an albatross," Sari Gadish added. "We wanted to make sure he had the best chance he could of survival, since he'd chosen the body of a *moli* in which to spend his next life."

Sophie scanned Gadish's face for any sign of humor; there was none. Clearly, the woman believed this.

A Maui Police Department blue and white cruiser bumped over the rutted road and pulled up in the lot; Lei shaded her face with a hand to see who was at the wheel, and then grinned, trotting over to the car as it parked. "Abe! What are you doing out here?"

Sophie remained standing awkwardly with the board members as Abe Torufu, a massive Tongan man she'd met at one of Lei's house parties some years ago, unfolded himself from the low-slung sedan to stand. He was a detective Lei'd partnered with during a brief stint on the island's bomb squad.

"Hey, Lei." Torufu gave Lei a brief greeting hug. "Had to come out to the emergency meeting of the Albatross Sanctuary board. I'm the treasurer of our little nonprofit."

"Why didn't you tell me?" Lei punched Torufu in the arm, and then shook her hand as if her fist had hit a boulder. "I wouldn't have taken this on if I knew you were already involved."

"That's my fault." Dr. Powers waved to attract their attention. "I asked Abe to find another cop down at the station who'd care about the albatrosses and rope them in to help with our cause."

Torufu grinned, unrepentant. "I shunted the request to your e-mail and look who you brought over to help! Sophie, the techno wonder woman." He strode over and clapped Sophie on the back. "The birds and I thank you for coming all this way, Sophie."

"Wait a minute." Lei put her hands on her hips. "Now we've got too many cooks in the kitchen. I want to know why you're involved with the sanctuary, Abe, and why you dragged me in, too. Omura forbade me to work on this case."

The big man sobered and folded his arms on his massive chest. His face assumed a remote expression that put Sophie in mind of an Easter Island statue. "The *moli* are my *'aumakua*. My sacred family ancestral guardian."

Sophie was aware of the Hawaiian belief in *'aumakua* as family deities; it made sense that as a Polynesian, Torufu shared this belief.

"Why do you need our help, Abe?" she asked.

"We want those eggs back, alive," Torufu said. "We need more investigators on board. And today, I've got a project for us." He rubbed big hands together in excitement. "Sari and Mahmoud paid for security cameras for the sanctuary, which we've needed from the

14

Sun beat down on Lei's head and wind tried to snatch her cap off at the Maui Albatross Sanctuary. Lei glanced over at Sophie, worried about her friend's response to Torufu's bold statement about needing help installing surveillance cameras; Abe had really overstepped himself.

But Sophie said nothing about Torufu's ambush of her time and professional services. Instead, she stepped forward, leaned over into his cruiser's trunk, and grabbed a heavy-looking metal toolbox and a couple of the surveillance cameras, still in their packaging. "Let's get going on this project. It's going to be a bit of work."

Soon the rest of them had filled their arms with cable wire, photovoltaic battery attachments that would run the cameras, and more boxed camera nodes. Torufu donned the heaviest load of all, a backpack to which he'd strapped two sturdy folding ladders. The little cavalcade moved out from the parking lot to the familiar trail over the dunes.

Lei came abreast of Sophie and handed her an extra water bottle. "I'm sorry. I had no idea Abe was planning to take advantage of your visit like this."

"If I was offended, I would've said so," Sophie said. "It's flattering, really. Torufu knows I can get the job done effectively."

They soon reached the albatross sanctuary area. Unlike its sister reserve on Oahu, the Maui reserve was not open to the public. A heavy padlock and chain locked a gate in the high chain-link fence. Dr. Powers unlocked the portal, and the group filed inside the sanctuary area.

The albatrosses were not visible from where they stood, but the area was thick with *naupaka* bushes, *haole koa*, and umbrellalike heliotrope trees, all typical growth in sandy areas of Hawaii.

"I hope you bought enough cameras and cable and batteries," Mahmoud Gadish said. "But if not, we'll pay for more."

"Hopefully I brought all we'll need. I thought we should place two camera nodes near the gate," Torufu said. "One on either side. But we need to install them along the entire length of the fence, to be honest. Perpetrators could use wire cutters and come in anywhere. Sophie, are you familiar with this brand of security camera? Can you tell us its range and where we should position them?"

Lei watched as Sophie examined the specifics on the cardboard box she held. "I'm familiar with this device. We need to put one about every fifty feet along the fence, unless you want to double the length and just try to catch someone who might not notice them," Sophie said. "You have twenty cameras here, each with a solar battery. We'll need to run the cable to connect the cameras all along the top of the fence. This project would go best if those who are not installing move ahead along the fence line and cut back the brush, so that we can gain access with the ladders."

Lei frowned at Torufu. "Have you measured how long the fence is?"

"Yep. We should have enough to do most of it," Torufu said. Everyone scattered to their individual tasks.

Lei, Sophie, and Torufu worked on the specifics of installing the cameras. Sophie wired each node to the posts at the top of the fence, installing their solar batteries, and then handed the power cable to Torufu to unspool. Lei used the second ladder to secure the cable to the top of the fence with plastic zip ties.

The three board members, equipped with pruning tools, moved along the fence ahead of them, clearing the overgrown brush so that the team could reach the fence. It was hot, tiring work; the sun would have been merciless if not for steady onshore winds blowing in from the sea. Even so, Lei enjoyed doing something physical outdoors for a change.

A loud hum distracted them; Lei glanced up to see a large black drone headed their way. She poked Abe on his rock-hard shoulder. "I thought those flying menaces weren't allowed in the sanctuary area."

"They aren't." The three investigators, temporarily near the bottom of Sophie's ladder to unwrap a new camera and battery, watched the approach of the buzzing craft.

Sophie narrowed her eyes, sheltering them with a hand. "That's a weaponized version! I recognize the model."

"What the hell is something like that doing out here?" Torufu exclaimed.

"I don't know, but it can't be good," Sophie said. "Everyone, take cover!"

"Get down!" Lei shouted, reaching for her police issue Glock. "That means you, Dr. Powers!" The intrepid biologist stood with her binoculars to her eyes, apparently trying to find out more about the incoming device.

Sari and Mahmoud, nearest Sophie, crouched beneath the ladder as Sophie descended the last few rungs and jumped to the ground. Lei crouched behind a boulder, tracking the drone with her weapon as it continued to approach.

The device was larger than any she'd seen, about the size of a large-sized pizza—but there the resemblance ended. Square, with four heavy-duty propellers at its corners, the thing resembled a miniature helicopter more than any other recreational flying device she'd ever seen.

The drone was twenty or so feet away when it emitted a sudden spitting sound.

Sophie dove away from the ladder to land headfirst into a stand of *haole koa*—and Sari cried out in pain. "Something hit me!"

The mini-aircraft shot forward suddenly to hover over the ladder—and Lei stood up from behind the rock just as Torufu stepped out from the stand of *haole koa* he'd sheltered behind. Both opened fire on the airborne threat at the same time.

The drone sparked, circling wildly, and then veered to crash into the bushes.

Lei glanced over at Torufu. "Nice shooting."

"Was just going to say the same, but the damn thing was hard to miss."

Lei holstered her weapon and hurried over to where Mahmoud Gadish cradled his injured wife. Sophie knelt beside her, examining a dart that protruded from Sari's bare, tanned upper arm.

"Wake up, darling. I'm here." The woman appeared to have fainted—her husband was lightly slapping her cheeks.

Sophie turned to Lei; her face had gone pale with stress and her eyes were wide and haunted. "I think she's been poisoned. Call for backup and an ambulance!"

Torufu approached. "Got it," he said, fumbling with his phone.

Lei frowned and grabbed Sophie by her biceps. "What haven't you been telling me, Sophie?"

15

Lei's eyes had gone dark and hard with anger; her voice was pure cop as she rapped out, "What haven't you been telling me, Sophie?"

There was so much she hadn't told Lei, and now it might have killed this poor woman, just a bystander.

But Sari Gadish's life might still be saved.

Sophie turned back to the fallen Albatross Sanctuary board member. She grabbed the dart protruding from the woman's shoulder carefully and pulled it out. She examined it: a classic tranquilizer needle with tiny plastic guidance fins and a fluid-filled bulb, now empty, that had injected upon impact.

Dr. Powers squatted beside Gadish and reached in with a rolled bandanna in her hands. "Let's tie off her arm and keep some of whatever was in that dart from circulating."

The biologist wrapped the kerchief around Sari's upper bicep and tightened it so brutally that the unconscious woman twitched. "Hopefully that slows it down."

Sophie was relatively sure the dart was much more deadly than a tranquilizer; why would that expensive drone be doing anything but trying to kill someone? Sophie was the likely target, not Sari Gadish.

"We must hydrate her, help her body purge the poison. Mr. Gadish, hold her upright. Let's get as much fluid into her as we can."

89

Sophie unscrewed the cap of the water bottle Lei had given her. "Pinch her jaw to open her mouth."

Mahmoud Gadish, still crooning endearments, propped up his wife in his arms and squeezed the sides of her jaw with one hand; her slack mouth fell open. Sophie poured water in carefully, stroking the woman's throat to elicit a swallow response.

Sari gulped—once, twice. Some of the water spilled out of her mouth, but more was going in than she was losing.

"Ambulance is on the way. Let's move her to the parking lot for pickup," Torufu said. "I can carry her, Mahmoud, if you'll let me."

The short, stout man nodded—though Sari was petite, clearly that task was too much for him physically. Torufu reached down and scooped Sari into his arms with ease.

"Dr. Powers, keep pouring water into her as they go," Sophie directed, handing the bottle to the biologist. The older woman nodded and the little cavalcade, led by Torufu carrying Sari, headed for the gate. Sophie was left with Lei.

She turned to face her friend. "Let's go get that drone. I'll tell you what I know on the way."

"You'll tell me now."

Sophie had never seen Lei so angry; heat seemed to shoot from her narrowed eyes and her hands had balled into fists.

"My mother is trying to kill me."

Lei's mouth dropped ajar, and her eyes widened. "What the hell?"

"She wants my children," Sophie said. "And revenge on me for giving her over to the CIA a few years ago. But—I never would have come here and endangered you or these people if I'd thought she'd make a move on me here."

"You told me your mom was an agent with that shady Thai organization, but not that she was after you. Why?"

"Before I say anything more, can we get the drone? Then we can check its range. The operator might still be close by and maybe we can . . ."

Lei spun to head into the brush instead of replying, her weapon drawn.

Sophie had never felt so naked without a firearm as she did right now.

Why had she let down her guard? And what might be happening at her house right now?

Sophie pulled her phone out, just in time for a branch Lei had pushed through to whip back and smack her in the face.

"Offspring of a warty pox-ridden swine!" Eyes watering, Sophie fumbled to find her Favorites button to call Armita and check on the children.

"You have no right to swear if you've brought this down on us without a truthful word to me about what's really going on in your life!" Lei pushed past another branch that whipped back and caught Sophie on the arm.

Sophie lost her temper at the second sharp sting. "I'm sorry, Lei. I'm sorry! Do you think I want to be in this situation?" Adding to her stress, the call wouldn't go through.

They'd reached the area where the drone had gone down; one of the device's propellers was still whirling. It had caught in the branches of a *haole koa* tree; the aircraft had a menacing aspect communicated by the weapons turret on its belly, whose blinking red eye gave both women reason to pause as they approached.

"Do you think it can see us?" Lei stopped at the edge of the clearing, stepping behind some tree cover.

"Not likely. Most of these are piloted remotely, and whoever was running it must know it's down. This version has a long range—close to a mile. Whoever was piloting it is likely gone by now. Let me go fetch it."

But Lei grabbed Sophie's arm as she tried to move past. "What if it's got a motion sensor or is booby-trapped? We should get Torufu. He's our bomb squad guy. He can check and see if it's okay to approach. Let's go see how Sari is doing and bring him back."

Sophie tightened her jaw; it was unlikely the drone posed any further danger, but she wasn't the one in charge. "If you think so."

"I think you better start talking and telling me what's really going on in this situation." Lei turned Sophie around and gave her a little push, pointing her toward the parking area. "Walk and talk, Soph."

"A lot of what's going on is classified," Sophie said. "That's why I didn't tell you."

"And you led a killer over here to Maui to hurt an innocent bystander," Lei said. "Good choice."

Sophie bit back her protestations—there was no defense because Lei was right. She felt horrible. She pushed back through the same brush they'd just come through, filling in the gaps in Lei's knowledge. "We chased my mother and almost caught her recently."

"Why didn't you tell me?" Lei growled. "I thought you were my friend!"

"I couldn't! Why bother you? It was awful, and my load to bear!" Sophie tripped over a root, but caught herself, refocusing. "After Connor killed her lover, the Master in Thailand, Pim Wat escaped from the fortress. Connor pinned the assassination on Pim Wat as far as the ninjas over there were concerned; he didn't know that killing the Master would make him have to take the position, but he was stuck. Meanwhile, the international task force that includes the CIA negotiated with Connor to take Pim Wat prisoner in return for immunity. A month ago, Connor found her in Paris. We sent over my colleague Pierre Raveaux and a team, but she got away again." Sophie finished the story that had ended at Phi Ni and her reunion with Connor as lovers.

They arrived at the parking lot just in time to see an ambulance pull away, its lights flashing, followed by the dun-colored pickup Dr. Powers drove. The Mercedes SUV that the Gadishes had arrived in remained, along with Torufu's police cruiser and Lei's Toyota truck.

Torufu strode toward them, his brow furrowed.

"How is Sari doing?" Sophie asked.

"Barely hanging on." Torufu shook his head gravely. "We told the EMTs we thought she might be poisoned. Her pulse was slow and irregular. They got an IV and a catheter into her immediately. Mahmoud rode with her in the wagon and Powers went to keep an eye on the situation—but it looks bad."

Sophie's gut clenched. "I'm so sorry."

"Me too. But hey—I thought you ladies were going after the drone?"

Sophie tensed, wondering how much of her outlandish story Lei was going to tell the big man; but her friend only described the reasons they hadn't yet retrieved the device, and asked him to come check it out. "The thing was still live when we left it, though downed. Do you have any of your bomb equipment with you?"

"You're in luck because I drove my cruiser out here. I always keep a suit and some tools in the trunk. Never know when I'm going to get a deactivation call." Torufu returned to his vehicle and popped the roomy trunk. "I'm not going to get into the suit until I know if it's needed—it's heavy and hot."

"Boy, do I remember that." Lei blew a curl off her forehead. "I'll never forget how steamy it was inside that outfit when I was working bomb squad with you. How about Sophie and I carry it out there, just in case?"

"You've got a deal." Torufu hefted a heavy steel toolbox and a long collapsible pole out of the trunk. "We can get started with these things."

Lei handed Sophie a plastic bin that held the lower half of the blast-resistant suit, which included the footwear.

"I need a minute to try to contact Armita, my nanny, about the attack," Sophie said. "I couldn't get a signal inside the preserve."

"Hurry up. Catch up with us after you make your call." Lei turned to follow Torufu, carrying the other bin containing the top half of the suit.

Sophie wasn't forgiven.

She held the phone, toning as it rang, to her ear as she watched the two Maui Police Department detectives hike toward the gate into the sanctuary.

The phone rang and rang, but Armita never picked up. Sophie left a message warning her that Pim Wat had made a move. She then texted her security team at the house to go on high alert. Once she had confirmation that they would coordinate with Armita, she slid the phone back into her pocket.

If she could find the drone's operator, she might be able to redeem herself. And if that operator was Pim Wat? So much the better.

16

Lei led Torufu through the rough terrain she had just traversed with Sophie, ending at the small clearing where the drone had landed in the *haole koa* tree.

She stopped just inside the vegetation cover and pointed to the downed craft. The red light was still blinking, and the same propeller whirling. "There."

Torufu lifted a pair of binoculars to his eyes and adjusted them, scanning the object. "I don't see anything obvious indicating that it's rigged, but the ocular sensor still appears to be live; it could still fire one of those darts." He turned back to Lei with a gusty sigh. "I should probably put on the suit."

Lei lifted off the lid of the plastic bin, and Torufu picked up the blastproof helmet with its heavy faceplate and the upper body protection jacket. "Where's Sophie with the bottom half?"

Lei frowned as she turned to look back down the trail, but no movement stirred the bushes. "She must've got tied up on the phone."

"Well, I'll just use the rod to give it a poke when I'm close enough. The weapons turret is around shoulder height; I doubt the thing would hit my legs if it went off, so just the top half of the suit should be fine."

Lei wasn't thrilled with that idea. "Just hang on. Let me run back and see if I can get the bottom half."

She turned and pushed as fast as she could through the heavy vegetation toward the parking lot. She still hadn't seen Sophie by the time she reached the highest dune—and then, she spotted the plastic bin resting on the ground just inside the sanctuary's gate.

Maybe Sophie'd had to use the bushes for a pee?

"Sophie!" Lei raised her voice and cupped her hands around her mouth. "Where are you?"

No reply. Off in the distance, the wail of approaching sirens—backup on its way.

Lei ran on to the top of the rise that looked down into the parking lot, but Sophie was nowhere to be seen.

Her friend had gone off to look for the drone operator by herself. Unarmed.

"Damn that woman!" If only Lei could use some of Sophie's exotic curses to express herself, but all she had were tired old American cusswords that she let fly to vent her frustration and fear.

Lei scooped up the bin containing the bottom half of the suit. She ran down the path carrying the heavy bin and calling on a lifetime of physical fitness to get her to Torufu's side in a hurry.

"Sophie's gone. I think she's looking for the operator by herself," Lei said as she reached the big man, who had taken the headgear off to examine the drone in its resting place again with the binoculars.

"That's not smart." Torufu was still examining the device.

"Do you need me to help you?" Lei dropped the bin containing the bottom half of the protective outfit at Torufu's feet. "I want to go find her."

"You bet I do, partner. No sense having you both going off half-cocked into the bushes. Sophie's chance of finding the perp is two clicks off none." Torufu set down the binoculars and pulled on the heavy pants and boots contained in the bin, then donned the headgear with Lei's help. "Here goes nothing."

Lei forced herself to breathe calmly as Torufu, holding the metal probe, approached the potential bomb that was the downed flying device. She'd spent six months working closely with Abe as the island's bomb squad team, before Captain Omura concluded that Lei wasn't temperamentally suited for the job. In all that time, deactivating potential explosives had never become easier for her, though Abe Torufu seemed to thrive on the challenge.

Halfway across the open area in front of the drone, Torufu opened the long metal rod with its gripper mechanism and extended it to full length. He used the twenty-foot rod to probe the drone.

Nothing happened: no explosion, no hissing spit of a poisoned dart.

Torufu aimed the rubber-tipped grip mechanism at the small turret on the bottom of the drone and touched an embedded button. The remaining propeller stopped. The blinking red light went out.

"Looks like I've got it deactivated." Torufu's voice was muffled by the headgear.

He approached the device and looked it over from close proximity. Still behind cover, Lei couldn't help bouncing on the balls of her feet, eager to try to go find Sophie, and yet terrified for her partner. Torufu's calm was his strength in this kind of task.

"I'm checking it for booby-trapping," Torufu said aloud. He examined the device from all angles, then walked around it, gently untangling the flexible branches of the *haole koa* before he lifted the device carefully out of the tree, without jostling, and set it on the ground. "Let's leave it here for now. I'll take it in to the lab in a containment device. We can check out the manufacturer and see if we can find any fingerprints or other clues."

"Roger that, Abe," Lei said.

"Can you get the caution tape out of my kit? Wouldn't want one of our uniforms to accidentally trigger something."

"You got it, partner." Lei opened his toolbox and took out the roll of crime scene/caution tape. "I thought you said you had equipment in your car?"

"No containment boxes. Those things weigh a lot and take up a lot of room. I keep one in the bomb squad truck," Torufu said. "This is good enough for the moment. I don't think this thing poses an active threat now that it's turned off." He ran the tape around the clearing, then returned to Lei. He took off his helmet. "Now, what are we gonna do about your missing friend?"

"I'm gonna find her, then kill her myself," Lei said.

"She'll turn up with empty hands and you can commit homicide then. We'll have a whole team out here looking in just a few minutes." Torufu indicated the now silent sirens with his head—their police backup must have reached the parking lot. Sure enough, Torufu's radio squawked, asking for updates.

Lei helped Torufu repack the suit in the bins, leaving it for when he moved the device to a containment canister.

"I want to know why Sophie thinks she's a better person to find the drone operator than we are," Torufu said as they approached the cluster of cruisers that had pulled up and parked in the lot. "Why would she take off like that without even a vest or a weapon?"

"I have an idea," Lei said, but it was going to be a long story, and a lot of it couldn't be told right now. "Let's get those uniforms out there looking."

17

After dropping off the bin containing the blast suit inside the fenced reserve area, Sophie returned to the sandy rise from which she could see in all directions.

The drone's range was close to a mile. Having operated one of them herself during a Security Solutions case, Sophie'd experienced how hard it was to pilot one of the devices using only the video tablet and hand switches. Because of the challenges, the operator would have chosen the highest ground they could find to get a visual of the device as they were flying it, as well as using the control panel for maneuvering. Entering the fenced area of the sanctuary would only have slowed them down; they wouldn't have bothered with breaking in.

Sophie shielded her eyes from the sun, squinting as she evaluated the topography.

She scanned until she spotted a high point near the end of the beach where black lava rock bluffs provided a natural barrier that ended the nesting area. A narrow maintenance trail on the exterior of the tall chain-link fence defining the albatross sanctuary appeared to head in the right direction.

Sophie bent over to tighten her shoelaces, then tugged down her cap and set off at a run.

As she jogged, Sophie's mind whirled with questions. How had the drone operator found her and followed her out here? Was there a surveillance device on her, Lei, or Lei's truck somewhere? She'd frisked herself in the parking lot and opened and disabled her phone, finding nothing.

The operator could just have tracked her phone's signal and been monitoring that, but she didn't have a spare burner to be able to ditch it right now . . .

All these questions would have to be answered, but finding out where the drone operator was, or had been, was the best way to help the investigation right now. If there was any chance at all that the drone operator was Pim Wat, Sophie would be the one to bring her down.

Sophie covered the mile or so of terrain quickly and arrived at the most likely vantage point—a lava cliff among hardy ironwood trees.

Once she reached the ridge, Sophie cast about, walking slowly back and forth until she found a view spot that had been used by either maintenance people or surfers to check the wave break just off the black boulders.

The ever-present wind soughed through the ironwoods' long, soft needles and tugged at Sophie's hat, threatening to flip it off. She moved into the bare area between the trees, searching the ground as carefully as a visual bloodhound.

Recent shoeprints not yet filled by the constantly moving sand.

Four small indentations indicated a folding camping stool.

Behind one of the grayish ironwood tree trunks, the stub of a slim unfiltered cigarette, a French brand uncommon in Hawaii.

The operator had been here. He or she had sat quietly, smoking, and directed the drone to attack their party. Whoever it had been had plenty of time to get into position while she and Lei were taking their informal tour in the beginning.

But that person wasn't Pim Wat.

The shoe prints were too big, and Pim Wat had never been a smoker. "Filthy habit," she'd said when she'd caught Sophie as a teen with a cigarette. Her delicate nostrils had flared with contempt. "Ages the skin like nothing else."

"And heaven knows you'd never do anything to age your skin, Mother," Sophie muttered. She squatted and reassembled her phone. She took photos of the cigarette *in situ*, the shoe prints, and the indentations from the stool. She set a GPS pin in the location and sent all the info via text to Lei, with a message:

"I found where the drone operator sat. I'm sorry, but for safety reasons I must get myself home ASAP. The drone operator was not my mother, the key thing I wanted to rule out—but that doesn't mean this attack wasn't related to my problems with her. I beg that you keep this part of the investigation quiet for a little longer and let me and my team try to find the perp behind the attack with all the resources we can bring to bear."

Lei was not going to be happy. This action might even cost Sophie Lei's friendship, but this was the best she could do to avoid the risk of getting caught up in their investigation and detained on Maui indefinitely.

Sophie straightened up, taking a last look around that included a regretful scan of the albatross sanctuary where Lei and Torufu were no doubt dealing with the drone.

Sophie jogged along a faint trail in the direction of the road, the phone to her ear as she called for her own backup in the form of the Security Solutions jet. When transport was on its way, she took the phone apart again even as it lit up with messages from Lei.

She couldn't afford to regret her choices. She had to survive to protect her family. Once she'd guaranteed that, she'd turn her attention to neutralizing Pim Wat.

Lei would forgive her for all that had gone down today, or she would not.

🌴

Two hours later, the Security Solutions jet took off with Sophie and Lono Jones sitting side by side in the leather seats. "I hope you know what you're doing," Jones said, eyes on the closed cockpit door as g-forces pushed them back into their cushy leather seats. "You burned a lot of folks at MPD today by taking off like this, especially if the victim dies."

Sophie folded her lips tightly over any response; there was nothing to say, because Jones was correct. She stared out the window at the lush green jungle of Haiku below them, the turquoise sea trimmed in lacy foam and yellow beach, the vast purplish bulk of Haleakala volcano wreathed in clouds.

When would she see this jewel of an island again?

Her heart hurt at the thought of losing Lei's friendship—but she had to get home to her babies and make sure they were safe.

The jet curved north toward Oahu; they'd be on the ground soon.

Jones cleared his throat. "There are probably a bunch of calls you should make."

Sophie roused herself from the morass of regret and second-guessing with difficulty; the talons of depression already had a grip on her brain, and thinking had become difficult.

That, or she was dehydrated from running for miles from the albatross sanctuary to the Kahului airport downtown without hydration. "Got any water?"

"I'm sure there's something around." Jones tossed aside his seat belt and rose to rustle around in the plane's galley—they'd taken off too quickly to have any crew on board but the pilot and Jones himself. He returned with two plastic bottles of water. "You look done in."

"I am." Sophie unscrewed the water bottles and applied herself to drinking one of them to the bottom. She set it aside when empty. Her stomach swishing uncomfortably with liquid, she extended a hand. "I asked you to bring me a new phone."

"I stopped at the drugstore on the way to the airport in Honolulu to buy you a burner. It's nothing fancy but it will do for now. I already programmed in a bunch of your important numbers."

Sophie met his hazel gaze with gratitude. "Thank you, Lono. This helps a lot. Can I get a bit of privacy for a phone call?"

"Sure. I'll go kick back in the bedroom. Keep an eye on the clock, though—it's only a half-hour flight."

"Duly noted."

Sophie waited until Jones disappeared into the jet's bedroom. She drank the second bottle of water, then opened the phone and typed in Connor's number from memory.

18

Connor sat at his bank of computer monitors, attending to administration for the Yām Khûmkạn. The ancient organization had its fingers in a surprising number of lucrative businesses and keeping it all going took time and effort. Though he'd found a measure of freedom from his responsibilities as the Master within the immediate walls of the fortress by delegating leadership to the diverse heads of different disciplines, he was still the functional CEO, and that position took more time, effort and planning than he'd been aware of when he stepped into the former Master's shoes.

Connor's private cell phone rang. He picked up.

"Connor. It's Sophie."

"Sophie!" A surge of emotion flooded his system. Surprise, delight, and a fillip of apprehension filled him—this was a new phone and her voice sounded tense. "How's everything on Oahu?"

"I've been on Maui for a case, and—everything has gone to Hades in a wheelbarrow."

"You mean—hell in a hand-basket? What's going on?" It had been ages since Sophie misused an American idiom. Her voice sounded hoarse, exhausted.

"Pim Wat's trying to take me out first this time."

Connor needed a moment to absorb this. He stood up from the

ergonomic stool where he'd been sitting at his workstation and walked over to the single window. He stared down into a courtyard where the ninjas of the Yām Khûmkạn were drilling below.

Waning daylight cast long shadows that danced beside the moving men in abstract patterns. A scarlet jungle bird flew by, sunset catching on its black-trimmed wings. He focused on these things as he listened to Sophie's tale and cursed when she came to the part about the drone attack. "You never should have gone to Maui!"

"I know that now. I didn't expect this kind of attack from her in broad daylight, with a drone of all things! But she wasn't piloting the device; it was likely one of Mendoza's assassins."

Connor bit back objections as Sophie described going after the operator herself, alone and unarmed. There was no point in protestations after the fact; she'd done what she'd thought best and emerged unscathed.

But the risks she'd taken left him chilled.

Connor returned to the computers and put on his headphones, connecting the Bluetooth. "Let me check on how the victim is doing. Your situation is going to get very complicated if the woman dies."

"Her name is Sari Gadish, and she is a lovely person," Sophie's voice wobbled. "I'm just sick that this happened. I had to tell Lei what the real situation is with my mother. When I left Maui, I asked her to keep it quiet so that we can pursue the drone operator ourselves, but I have no guarantee that she will. If she brings Pim Wat's name into the MPD investigation, that will mean the FBI will get involved."

Connor's fingers had been a blur on the keys since he sat down as he used his Ghost software program to hack into the MPD's database. "I found the police report on the drone attack. Looks like it was submitted by one Abraham Torufu."

"Yes. Abe Torufu is Lei's friend. He was working with Lei to make sure the drone wasn't armed when I left. He's the island's bomb deactivation technician. He's also on the board of the Albatross Sanctuary, and he's the one that drew Lei in on their case involving missing eggs. I came because it seemed like the two cases might be connected." Sophie sighed, and she sounded infinitely tired. "I was able to verify that Armita and the children are okay. My security team at the Kailua house is on high alert. I plan to work from home until this latest threat is under control."

"Please confirm when you're safely in your home." Connor had a new thread to follow online, but he'd been cultivating the ability to focus on more than one task at a time and this posed no challenge.

"Didn't you send Raveaux to Bali to look for Pim Wat?"

"I did, and he and his team are overdue to check in." Connor squinted at the monitor; he'd used a link in the report on the drone attack victim to follow the data to the hospital database. His eyes widened as he read her status. "Sari Gadish is deceased. She died a few hours after arrival at the hospital. Your drone attack is now a homicide."

"Oh no!" Sophie's voice broke. "I can't handle this."

She ended the call abruptly, and the silence after she did so was as painful as a bruise.

His beloved was hurting.

Connor was half a world away, unable to comfort her. If only he could take her in his arms and provide a safe place for her and the babies. "Damn Pim Wat to hell. May she rot for eternity, tormented by the souls she's taken."

Sophie's elaborate curses were wearing off on him, but no words were enough.

Nothing but finding and stopping Pim Wat could alleviate this pain. He needed to get in touch with Raveaux in Bali.

Connor's entire spy network was looking for Pim Wat, but now that he had this information, he could both widen and focus the search; Pim Wat must be working with one of Mendoza's operatives again, as Sophie had speculated.

But what if the attack on Maui was a diversion, part of a multi-pronged assault?

What if Pim Wat was going after Sophie's house—or coming after Connor here at the compound—herself?

In fact, that was the likeliest scenario.

"Divide and conquer," Connor murmured. "That's what she'd do."

He reached for the silk rope that rang a bell for Feirn. He would put the fortress on high alert, and then he'd get in touch with Raveaux.

Connor moved quickly to rally his troops and get the fortress locked down—but when he tried Raveaux on his private line, the device went straight to voicemail.

A cold unease tightened the notch where Connor's skull met his spine.

Why hadn't the Frenchman and the ninjas he'd sent to meet him checked in?

They were probably in transit somewhere. He'd try again later.

Meanwhile, it was time for Connor to take that top secret surprise trip to Oahu that he'd planned. All he had to do was alert his men and the pilots. Early tomorrow morning would be perfect for his departure for Hawaii.

Sophie needed him and nothing but holding her would do.

19

Day 6

Pierre Raveaux stood beside the razor wire-topped gate at the metal warehouse he'd rented on the outskirts of Paris. Located in a seedy area on the outskirts of the city, sandwiched between a couple of decaying brick factory buildings, the corner was deserted. Wan yellow security lights lit the battered cobblestone street; Raveaux had made sure they pointed outward, away from the building.

Right on time, the plain white transport van he'd secured drove up to the gate with Rab at the wheel. Raveaux rolled the chain-link barrier open, and the vehicle drove in. He then shut it, securing the entry with a heavy chain and padlock.

He didn't want anyone to interrupt what was going on inside the warehouse.

Rab had jumped out of the driver's seat and pulled the lever on the rollaway door of the warehouse building; it lifted, and he moved quickly to drive inside.

Raveaux followed at a slower pace, steeling himself for what he had to do.

Enrique Mendoza was an evil man. He was responsible for an ungodly number of deaths. He didn't deserve to live, if justice were as simple as an eye for an eye.

But Raveaux wasn't in the habit of torturing people; he wasn't looking forward to what must be done now. Thankfully, his ninja companions from the Yām Khûmkạn seemed to have no such scruples.

Raveaux pulled the lever that lowered the door; it rattled down with a machine-gun sound and gave an echoing boom as its heavy lip hit the concrete floor.

Mendoza, hooded with a black bag, cringed and cried out as Sam, Rab's partner, wrestled him out of the van.

"What is this about?" Mendoza demanded in French; his voice muffled by the hood. "Do you know who you're dealing with? You've made a grave mistake."

Rab cocked his head toward the chair; Raveaux gave a brief nod, and Sam dragged the reluctant man toward the piece of furniture nailed to a square of heavy plywood. Beside it, on an overturned white paint bucket, a large marine boat battery was attached to a wire with a pair of clamps on the end. A single floodlight on a long cord dangled down to make a small, intense circle of light over the chair.

Raveaux stood in the darkness outside of the circle of light. He slid on a headset with a voice distorting microphone; Mendoza had met him socially not that long ago, and his voice could not be recognized.

"This is your last chance!" Mendoza yelled. "If you let me go now, I'll forget this happened. I'll let you go, no harm done. Don't be a fool!"

Sam put Mendoza in the chair. The man struggled, and Sam clouted him alongside the head as Rab secured him with ropes behind the chair back and at the ankles.

Rab finally withdrew the hood covering Mendoza's head, and the man gasped. "Who *are* you?"

Both Thai men wore their usual all-black *gi* with matching face masks; Raveaux approved of their identical, anonymously threatening appearances. The two ninjas melted back into the shadows to stand out of visible range, behind Raveaux.

Raveaux studied Mendoza as he sat bound on the chair, squinting into the darkness that surrounded his pool of illumination. The once dapper procurer of murder for hire turned his head and spotted the battery and clamps; sweat sprang out on his forehead, gleaming under the harsh lights. "I know you're out there," he said. "What do you want? I'm known to be reasonable. Bargain with me. Violence is beneath civilized men."

"If you were a civilized man, you wouldn't be in the line of work you're in." The voice distorter added a layer of menace to Raveaux's words.

"I own Kaleidoscope Tastemakers. We advise the choices of people in need of guidance regarding the more gracious things in life."

"Enough of the bull, Mendoza. That's not all your company does."

Mendoza digested that for a beat, then regrouped. "Do you represent a disgruntled client? I can make that right. Name a name; I'll eliminate them. No extra charge."

"We appreciate the offer, but it's one of your assets we want. Pim Wat. Give us her new name and location."

The beads of sweat on Mendoza's forehead increased in size, coalesced, and ran down his face in a sudden burst. "She'll kill me if I tell you."

"And we'll kill you after we make you suffer," Raveaux said. "Living a little longer is always the better choice." He nodded to his companions.

Rab and Sam moved on swift and silent feet out of the darkness, and Mendoza shrieked in terror as Rab seized the man's expensive, tailored shirt and ripped it open in a single yank, sending mother-of-pearl buttons flying. Sam picked up the clamps, knocking them against each other so that sparks flew.

"No! No!" Mendoza writhed and yanked at his bonds. "I'll tell you, but you must kill her when you find her. She can't be left alive, she's too dangerous!"

"We don't plan to let her get away," Raveaux said. "Help us, and we'll deal with her permanently."

"Pim Wat's in Greece!" Mendoza howled. "Corfu! She wanted somewhere warm. Her new name is Lisabetta Scartuzzi. She won't be expecting anyone; she's had more work done on her face."

Raveaux asked more questions, getting an address and specifics.

"Thank you, Monsieur Mendoza," he said at last. "You'll be driven to a secure location." He nodded to his comrades again.

Rab and Sam gagged and hooded Mendoza. Ignoring his muffled protests, they untied his feet but bound his arms and put him back in the van. Raveaux came over and pinned an envelope to the man's ruined shirt. "You're going somewhere safe," he said. "And don't worry. Pim Wat won't be able to reach you there."

Mendoza roared impotently from behind his gag.

Sam got in the back of the van with him and slid the door shut; Rab turned on the vehicle, and Raveaux went ahead to open the warehouse door.

He peered out as the metal portal was retracted.

The streets, lit by the sultry yellow lights, remained deserted. He jogged forward and unlocked the gate to the street.

The van drove through and turned left, headed for the downtown police station, where the envelope of evidence pinned to Mendoza's chest would make sure he went away for a long time for his crimes.

Raveaux walked back to the chair and wiped it down with a sanitary wipe. He rubbed down every surface their fingers had touched. He packed up the battery for disposal, putting it in a cardboard box. He turned off the lights and walked out to the front gate, then dropped the keys to the warehouse in the lockbox secured to the rolling portal for that purpose.

Finally, he walked to the corner and waited in the shadows against a building until the van drove back and picked him up again.

"Everything okay?" he asked Rab in English.

"Very good. That man roll to a police officer when Sam push him out," Rab said with a grin that revealed very white, pointed canines. "He not a problem anymore."

"I hope not, but sometimes men like him are connected. Friends in high places," Raveaux said.

Rab looked blank.

Raveaux shrugged. "To the airport, *s'il vous plait*. We're off to Greece."

20

Lisabetta frowned down at her phone, irritated by its insistent buzzing vibration as she was in transit. No one had this number except her boss, Enrique Mendoza. She had to take the call.

She reached into the little summer Prada bag resting on her lap and retrieved the phone as she gazed out the window of the rideshare she rode in. "Hello?"

An automated voice came on. *"To all my operatives: execute Alpha X. Hope to see you on the other side."*

The message ended.

"Thank you," Lisabetta said automatically. She slid the phone back into her purse

Mendoza was blown.

He'd ordered the complete liquidation of their operation in Paris, destruction of all records, and for everyone to get their go-bags and scatter.

She squeezed the purse tightly in reflexive frustration; she'd worked so hard to create a peaceful sanctuary and begin a new phase of her life with her grandchildren!

Maybe Mendoza wouldn't give her location up; she could always hope for that. Regardless, Lisabetta had a backup plan and an exit strategy. This news didn't change her current trajectory, only her destination.

But there was one very important thing she had to do.

She took out the phone once more, called a number, and input a code.

A slow smile curved Lisabetta's full lips as she put the device away.

Whoever had taken Mendoza and threatened her livelihood would regret it.

21

Lono Jones lifted a hand to wave goodbye as he pulled away in the Security Solutions SUV in which he'd driven Sophie home.

She turned from the departing vehicle to greet her home security team as Bill and Clement walked toward her from the guesthouse that served as their headquarters.

Her body ached with tiredness and depression; her whole being longed to go inside the house and greet Armita and her babies.

Even so, she'd timed her arrival to occur during the children's midday nap to create the least amount of disruption to their schedule while she dealt with security. Making sure the house was safe was the best way she could serve her family.

"Welcome home, Sophie," Bill said. Crinkles of good humor beside his blue eyes telegraphed genuine pleasure at the sight of her. Clement, his younger partner, merely ducked his head in greeting. "We're glad you're back."

"Thank you. We need to be alert for any drones or other aircraft." Sophie described the attack as succinctly as possible. "And I've just been informed that the victim, who I believe was hit by a dart by accident, has died. With that in mind, I'd like to see a plan to address any aircraft approaches to the estate."

"We'll consult with the team at headquarters," Bill said. Both men had gone serious at the terrible news.

"I think the camera surveillance devices embedded in the walls will help us spot incoming aircraft, but I want to know how we can disable any craft before they can get off a shot should this happen again," Sophie said. "Any unusual activity while I was gone? Anything from the device sweeps you've been doing?"

After Sophie had detected a camera in an expensive stuffed toy in the children's room, regular checks for bugging devices were done by the team as well as a manual inspection of anything coming into the house, no matter how innocuous.

"All clear so far," Bill said. "Do you want to bring a second security team on site?"

"Yes," Sophie said. "You both need to sleep, and I want two operatives awake and alert, on duty and around-the-clock for the foreseeable future."

"You got it, boss. Now go get some rest yourself. You look done in," Bill said.

Sophie nodded; she was still sweaty and sticky from her long run from the albatross sanctuary to the Maui airport, where she'd met Jones and the Security Solutions jet on the hot tarmac. "It's been a long day."

"We've got your back," Bill said.

Clement nodded. "You can relax now."

Sophie forced a smile and turned away. They meant well, but she wasn't reassured. Her mother ate men like Bill and Clement for afternoon tea.

Sophie walked across the lawn and pea gravel turnaround driveway to the entrance of the Mediterranean-style house. She scanned the gracious lava stone walls and the native Hawaiian plantings that softened them.

On the other side of one of the walls, a two-story mansion overlooked her estate; she'd never paid much attention to it until now—but didn't those windows have a good sniper angle to cover her property? The place wasn't occupied year-round, either, except by a caretaker.

An empty house with good sighting range was just the kind of setup that would render them vulnerable.

Sophie switched direction and headed back to the guesthouse.

Clement met her at the door. "Did you think of something?" His gaze was alert and respectful.

"I did. I'd like you to find out who's in residence next door and do a sweep through their house for any evidence of surveillance or trespass. Those upper windows could give an observer an advantage."

"We thought of that already," Clement said. "Bill and I have already talked to the caretaker. He's contacted the owners on the mainland for permission to search the house for evidence of any intruders. In the meantime, he did a walk-through and said he didn't see anything amiss."

"Thank you." Sophie didn't have to force a smile this time. "I appreciate the way you took initiative."

Her beloved nanny opened the front door as she approached. "Sophie, thank the gods," Armita murmured in Thai. She embraced Sophie in strong, wiry arms. "I'm so glad you're home."

Armita was not usually so demonstrative; she must have really been alarmed. Once more a stab of guilty regret shortened Sophie's breath. "I'm sorry to have worried you. How are the children?"

"They're fine." Armita released Sophie, only to grasp her by the shoulders in an almost painful grip, though she was much shorter and weighed no more than a hundred pounds. The nanny's deep-set eyes, so dark a brown as to be almost black, were haunted as they scanned Sophie's face. "Don't take any more chances. I cannot replace you as their mother."

"I know." Sophie drew Armita close, and for just a second, let herself lean on the smaller woman. "But if I were killed, you would care for the children, wouldn't you? You'd make sure they were safe and loved."

"Stop it." Armita stepped back from Sophie and flapped her hands angrily. "You may not go to that dark place in your head right now. I need you here, present, and sharp. The babies need you that way, too. When did you take your medicine last?"

Another pang of guilt; in the distractions of the previous week, Sophie had forgotten to take her antidepressant. Apparently, the pill was still needed. "I will take it right away."

"Yes. Go take a shower and your medication. I will fix you lunch, then you will lie down and rest. After that, you can see the children." Armita folded her arms on her narrow chest and glared at Sophie. "You must take care of yourself. You are no good to Momi and Sean depressed—or dead."

Sophie turned and headed down the hall toward the bathroom without a word; Armita was right.

Day 7

Sophie felt like she was swimming up through dark layers of heavy water as she woke from her nap and pushed the sleep mask up from her eyes. Disoriented, she stared at a slightly domed stucco ceiling trimmed in native *koa* wood. A ceiling fan with wooden blades and a pull cord hung motionless above her.

Gradually memory kicked in.

She was home, in her new bed, after the disastrous trip to Maui.

Sophie spread her arms, sliding them over the smooth cotton of the plain white matelassé comforter. She hadn't slept here long enough for the room or the space to resonate with familiarity yet.

She turned her head and tracked around the room; the furnishings were period pieces from the 1940s chosen to match the house's era, and made of *koa* wood: a dresser, a comfy rocker she sat in with Sean, a vanity with a mirror and a little stool where Momi loved to sit and primp. A few vintage framed Hawaii travel posters brightened the walls; a single window, framed in filmy curtains, let in the slanted orange light of sunrise.

"*Oh, son of a flea-bitten dog,*" she muttered, tossing off the light coverlet. She'd slept through to the next day!

Sophie removed her ear plugs and placed them in the bedside drawer. She might have slept too long, but the sleep had helped restore her. The encroaching fog of depression that had dulled her senses and sapped her energy seemed to have rolled back; she could breathe freely.

The house was quiet, but then the rooms were fairly soundproof. Armita likely had the children in the kitchen for breakfast. Sophie could take a few more moments to make sure her body and mind were back in working order. The children deserved her best.

Sophie went to the closet and took out a yoga mat. Hurrying now, she went through an accelerated series of ten Sun Salutations, feeling aches and pains from her exertions of the day before, and the fullness of breasts which hadn't been pumped in far too long. "Sean will be weaned before either of us are ready," Sophie muttered. "Enough of this."

She left the mat where it lay and hurried to the door, unable to wait one more moment to see her children.

Sophie stood in the doorway of the kitchen, yet unseen by her family.

She soaked in the sight before her: both dogs were curled together in their bed, Sean sat in his bouncer chair on the table, batting at a dangling toy with pudgy hands, and Momi was in her highchair with Armita beside her.

Armita handed Momi a cup of water, admonishing her in Thai to hold it with both hands. Sunrise gold light slanted in through the sliding glass door that opened onto the infinity pool with its newly installed safety fence. The smell of something tasty cooking on the stove filled the air.

"Hello, darlings," Sophie said, and stepped into pandemonium as the dogs boiled up from their bed and Momi and Sean yelled in excitement to see her.

Sophie made the rounds, kissing and hugging Momi first, then scooping Sean up out of his seat and sitting down in a kitchen chair with him to pat the dogs' heads, then facing Armita with a smile as she held the baby close. "Thank you, Armita. I needed the rest."

"Yes, you did. I've put on some restorative tea for you." Armita smiled back. "And I haven't fed the little man yet; I thought you'd want to."

"Yes," Sophie said simply, and she put the baby to her breast. Her whole being relaxed; she shut her eyes as the milk let down and her baby took his nourishment.

She wasn't leaving these precious ones again, no matter how urgent a case might be. They needed her more than anyone else could, and the truth was, she needed them just as much.

After the meal, Sophie took the children to the nursery to play while Armita cleaned up. Sean was rocking in his infant swing while Momi stacked blocks when Sophie's new phone rang. Sophie checked the display and picked up a forwarded call from Char Leong.

"Hello, Char." Sophie tucked Sean's blanket in around him as she sat on the floor beside the swing.

"Hey lady. How's tricks?"

Sophie frowned. "Um. I suppose you're asking me how things are going. Not well, in fact."

Leong's voice sobered. "I'm sorry to hear that. Did you mean personally, or with the case?"

"Both, I'm afraid. But I'd rather not get into it until you let me know why you're calling."

"Sure. Gotcha." Leong cleared her throat. "Thanks for the Stingray device. I identified the student whose art tipped off our counselor through matching the art to his submission to the Fabergé contest. It wasn't hard to follow the kid with the device. I hid in the library and was able to track two phones texting him harassing messages. The kid is being bullied, all right—browbeaten to keep quiet about the crime. He's in a bad way."

"That's a shame, though it doesn't excuse participating in such a deed."

"No joke. Anyway, after I tracked those two phones, I met with Ms. Dawnhorse and brought her up to speed. We've set up a meeting to interview the student tomorrow and try to get the names from him voluntarily. Can you come?"

"I have a personal situation and must stay home. I'd like to attend by video conference, though."

"That should be enough. We'll offer support as his mental health seems shaky. But he may not talk, so I wanted to give you the phone numbers and see if you could track down their owners."

"Yes, tracking the phones' owners is something I can do." Sophie stacked another block with an encouraging smile to Momi.

What, if anything, should she tell Leong about what had happened on Maui? She decided that nothing was better, for now. "Did you speak to the headmaster about what you've found out so far?"

"No, I thought I'd talk with you first."

"Good. I recommend you hold off apprising him until we have the three suspects clearly identified with proof of their involvement. I wouldn't want Dr. Ka'ula to overreact and cause them to cover their tracks by ditching their phones or other evidence. Right now, they have no idea we're tracking them, and I'd like to keep it that way."

"I'm dying to nail the ringleader. You should see the horrible things he's saying to this poor kid."

"We will get him, no doubt about it, unless he detects us and disposes of the phone and goes silent. Then we'll only have the one student's word, and that's not going to be enough for any kind of conviction."

"Dawnhorse's client's name is Bernard Valas. They call him 'Nard.' He's chubby, a loser of sorts. Not the brightest bulb in the box." Leong's voice was sad.

"That doesn't excuse what he did," Sophie repeated.

"I know. But I can see how he got sucked in, trying to appease the main bully and his sidekick."

Momi, losing patience with her mother's distraction, toppled the tower of blocks. One of them hit Sean on the leg, and the baby let out a surprised yelp. "Things are unraveling here. I must go," Sophie said. "Text me the numbers, and the date and time of the meeting tomorrow."

"Will do. Thanks, *chica*." Leong ended the call.

Sophie smiled as she tucked the phone into her pocket and dealt with her disgruntled children.

Char Leong had raised her spirits with this news. Once they had the perps who'd committed the Moli Massacre, those who'd stolen the albatross eggs on Maui couldn't be far behind; the two crimes had to be linked.

Later in the evening, when the children were asleep and Armita had gone to get some well-earned rest, Sophie settled in front of her computer monitors in her cool, neutral-toned office. Sighing with relief to be alone in her lovely office, Sophie engaged her rigs with a key fob. Prior to becoming a mother, she'd enjoyed music to work to; now, pure, uninterrupted silence was perfect.

Sophie punted the phone numbers Leong had picked up from the two perps into a tracking app and soon had the names and addresses of the two students. With that information, she was able to set her rogue DAVID program and Connor's Ghost program to work, pulling together everything recorded online about the three boys who appeared to have committed the massacre.

Bernard "Nard" Valas, the kid who'd been seeing Dharma Dawnhorse, had struggled with his weight for most of his life, if annual student photos were any guide. His grades were indifferent. He had flat feet that were unusually large. According to social media, gaming was his only real interest and outlet. An only child in a divorced family, he lived with a mother who traveled as a pharmaceutical salesperson and left him home alone for long stretches of time.

Sophie studied the boy's full, acne-riddled face, sad eyes, and downturned mouth. "You're the weak link of the gang," she murmured. "And may be at a real risk for suicide."

Sophie had done a deep dive into studying suicidality on one of her FBI cases. Nard's profile fit that of a candidate likely to succeed at a suicide attempt.

Neville "Kermit" Ignacio was "the sidekick," as Char Leong had characterized him. Short, wiry, and underdeveloped, Kermit appeared to be trying to prove himself by repeatedly trying out for athletics at which he didn't excel. The boy had average grades and intelligence, but a mean streak—a report of cruelty to a neighbor's dog had been filed a year ago by the pet's owners. This remained attached to his record, though obscured by adolescent privacy law.

Remo Ozawa, "Oz," was the ringleader of the three. Seventeen years old, he stood head and shoulders over the other two at six feet tall. His grades were exemplary. He was handsome and a track star; he too was a gamer.

That was likely how the three had become friends, though that term didn't really describe the twisted relationships that Sophie sensed bound the three boys.

She dug deeper, looking for dirt.

"Oz" came from a large, well-connected Big Island family, but he, too, was an only child. His mother had died when Oz was six, from a fall down the stairs that was ruled accidental. His father had brought the boy to Oahu after her death, when he started his own brokerage firm using his wife's death benefit as seed money. That business was now well-established with a seven-figure bottom line.

Hospital records for young Oz revealed a plethora of bruises, sprains, burns and broken bones that had been attributed to outdoor sports and adventure injuries.

Sophie frowned, leaning back in her chair to tap her chin with a finger. Though Oz himself had no record of misbehavior or law enforcement involvement, the profile she was reading matched that of an isolated child with an abusive parent, who'd turned to the abuse of others.

Ozawa's father could be the real bully of the scenario; and if she dug deep enough, she'd likely find medical records on the mother that matched those of her son.

Sophie got up, unsettled, and went to her pull-up bar to do some reps.

She was finding answers, but she wasn't liking them. It was easier to judge, to hate even, anyone who would attack helpless, beautiful birds like the Laysan albatross—but the truth of why might be complicated.

She returned to her desk and opened her phone to the contact she had for Dharma Dawnhorse. She wanted a psychology perspective on the three perpetrators, and some plan to address their crime in a way that would stop Oz's bullying and that of his father, Wendell Ozawa, even more.

Sophie's call to the counselor picked up on the fifth ring.

"Hello?" Dharma Dawnhorse had a resonant voice with a husky timbre to it. Sophie pictured the distinctive woman as she'd last seen her with her serious dark eyes, tattooed center part, and heavy braids.

"Ms. Dawnhorse? I'm sorry to bother you at home so late, but it's important. This is Sophie Smithson with Security Solutions. I'm calling regarding the counseling student you brought to our attention."

A pause as the woman digested this. "I see."

"Ms. Leong and I have been able to identify him and two other students whom we believe may have perpetrated the Moli Massacre."

Dawnhorse remained silent.

Sophie cleared her throat. "I would like to discuss the suspects and their psychological profiles with you, but I must be assured this conversation is held in the strictest confidence. The situation is very delicate."

"Of course it is. You have my word this discussion will go no further."

Sophie smiled. "I respect your commitment to the standards of your profession."

"Dr. Ka'ula contacted me to apologize for his harshness in our meeting. I believe I have you to thank for that." Dawnhorse's voice warmed.

"I merely gave him another perspective and he was wise enough to listen," Sophie said. "Back to our situation. Using technology that tracks cell phones, Ms. Leong and I were able to identify two students who are harassing your client, who we've identified as Bernard 'Nard' Valas."

Dawnhorse's breath hitched but she said nothing.

"It would greatly assist in moving the case forward if you were able to confirm that Bernard is the student you have concerns about," Sophie said.

"I must agree with identifying him to you because of his risk for suicidality," Dawnhorse said at last. "So yes, Bernard Valas is my client. I'm very worried about him."

"And if the threatening messages we pulled from the other students' phones are any indication, you should be," Sophie said. "Though I haven't personally seen the messages, Ms. Leong has, and she was upset by the content. We need to put a stop to this right away. I understand you have a meeting scheduled with your student and Ms. Leong for tomorrow?"

"We do."

"I will be joining by video. But for now, I'd like to tell you the names of the two students bullying him and see what you know about them and what may be their motives." Sophie told Dawnhorse about Kermit and Oz. "Are you aware of either of these boys?"

"I am not. But then, they are not the types that usually end up in my office."

"I believe that Remo Ozawa, who goes by 'Oz,' is the ringleader. I use a data mining internet program and I was able to develop a background on him." Sophie filled Dawnhorse in on Oz's likely history as a domestic violence witness and abuse victim. "Is there anything more you can find out about him to share with our team? Rumors at school, etcetera?"

"I will reach out to the eleventh-grade academic counselor and a few of the staff who work with him," Dawnhorse said. "Maybe I can pick up something before the meeting."

"Good. I look forward to tuning in with you." Sophie sat back a moment, covering her tired eyes with a hand, picturing Nard's face. "What have you done regarding Bernard's depressed state of mind?"

Dawnhorse gave a sharp inhale; Sophie's question hadn't been appropriately phrased. Sophie groped aloud. "I mean, to ensure his safety. I know firsthand how difficult depression can be; I've struggled with it myself since my teens. Suicide can assume a terrible allure in the right circumstances."

"I appreciate you saying that." Dawnhorse softened her tone. "I have contacted the boy's mother; the day I called, she came in and removed him, telling me she was taking him to a psychiatrist. The next day, when Bernard returned for his normal session, he said it was a waste of time. The man didn't give him fifteen minutes and just offered a pill, which he refused. He can't be forced to take medication, and in my opinion, though he may have a bit of a melancholy outlook due to many factors, this acute mental health crisis has its roots in the bullying and coercion he's undergoing. Medication won't solve that."

"Yes. I agree with you there." Sophie's gaze fell on the medicine bottle which she'd left at the monitor to help her remember to take it. She unscrewed the lid and shook a small white capsule into her palm; though her depression was triggered by events and circumstances such as the ones she was currently going through, in her case the disorder had an organic root cause in family history. "We need to put a stop to those boys' bullying as soon as possible and get to the bottom of what's bothering Bernard. When we do, hopefully he'll be better able to cope with what comes next."

"And what would that be?"

"Answering for his crime and taking responsibility for it," Sophie said. "He will need an advocate and a support when the time comes, and I'm glad he'll have you."

Sophie stared at her monitor after hanging up the phone. The silence in her office that had started off as such a balm had hardened into depressive loneliness.

She should call Connor back; she'd ended their conversation abruptly the last time they talked, overwhelmed by the news of Sari Gadish's murder.

But it wasn't Connor she missed right now—it was Pierre Raveaux.

He was the one who was a part of her daily life, a shoulder to lean on, a help with the children, a comfort. It couldn't hurt to reach out to let Pierre know what her mother had done—just in case Connor hadn't informed him.

Sophie found his number in her Favorites and pressed it.

The call went directly to voicemail; Sophie suppressed a stab of disappointment. "Pierre, it's Sophie. I hope you're well and safe. I called because an assassin, probably associated with Pim Wat and Mendoza, made an attempt on me while I was on Maui for a case. They used a drone and poisoned tranquilizer darts. A woman beside me was hit and killed." She paused, summoning her thoughts. "I don't like it that you've gone after Pim Wat. Please use the utmost care. I don't want to lose you. And I also want you to know that the children miss you, too. Stay safe."

She ended the call with a punch of her thumb, once again considering a call to Connor.

But no. Too many unanswered questions and unrequited longings lay in that direction.

She plugged her phone into a charger, turned off the office's lights, and headed to bed.

22

Day 7

Lei stood next to Torufu at the long steel table in the basement of the MPD building. The department's tech specialist had disassembled the drone after Torufu brought the device into the lab an explosive-resistant canister.

"The poison darts are the most interesting," the guy said. "They were adapted from commercially available tranquilizer darts. This whole firing apparatus was customized on this unit. Someone went to a lot of trouble to adapt this thing to fire these." The tech's eyes sparkled with enthusiasm as he tapped the darts, neatly lined up and labeled, with a gloved finger. "No fingerprints on them, unfortunately."

Torufu glanced at Lei. "There weren't any on that cigarette we recovered, either."

"This was a pro, obviously," Lei said.

Torufu held her gaze. "Why would a pro take out a nice lady like Sari Gadish?"

"That's what we have to find out." Lei frowned down at the remains of the drone on the table, frustrated that she'd decided not to share Sophie's outrageous story until she had to. "Is there anything else the drone itself can tell us?"

"Not that I can think of. It's an expensive device, heavy-duty, intended for law enforcement or military use. It's available to buy online from the manufacturer, but whoever adapted it knew what they were doing."

Torufu grasped Lei by the shoulder and squeezed; his message was clear: *we need to talk privately.* "Thanks. Box this up for evidence storage, will you?"

"You got it." The young man was still starry-eyed about his job, that much was clear as he hopped up to fetch a large evidence tag for his own and Torufu's signature.

Torufu dogged Lei's steps as she left the tech lab. "Your office or mine?"

"Pono is in our cubicle already this morning, so yours," Lei said.

Torufu had his own cubicle since he was now a one-man show as the island's bomb squad. The space, cluttered with tools and equipment, was familiar to Lei as she'd spent six months occupying it with him.

She took an empty stool Torufu kept under the desk for visitors and sat. "I take it you want to discuss the case."

"Just a bit." Torufu occupied his rump-sprung chair; it squeaked in protest under his weight. "Sophie had a reason for going after the drone operator's location and then taking off. She knows something. And if she knows something, you know something."

Lei rubbed gritty eyes, flashing back to yesterday. What a long day it had been! She'd received Sophie's message and hurried out to the location her friend had sent. She'd collected the cigarette butt and photographed the traces left by the drone's operator while Torufu was removing the drone in a bombproof container.

Then she'd got the call that Sari Gadish had died.

The case was now a homicide and getting Sophie's statement was important—but Sophie had disappeared, not replying to her calls and texts. Lieutenant Omura was one step away from issuing an arrest warrant, while Lei was reasonably sure her friend was no longer on the island at all.

Which meant she'd have to contact Oahu PD and send a cruiser out to Sophie's new house in Kailua—or she could fly over and buttonhole Sophie herself in her hideaway.

She'd decided to keep mum for the moment, hoping Sophie could do what she'd said she'd do—find the assassin more quickly than the rest of them could.

That hadn't happened, and Lei had run out of time. "Sophie may know something, yes."

"Damn right she does," Torufu growled. "Some friend she is, sneaking off without so much as a goodbye, let alone helping with our case."

"She did find the operator's launch site," Lei said. "But yeah, I agree. I can either send Oahu PD to her house in Kailua to get a statement or fly over there myself. I'm leaning toward the latter. She'll talk to me."

"Will she?" Torufu cocked his big square head, dark eyes hard. "She's hiding something. And back to my first statement: so are you."

Lei rubbed her eyes again. She'd hardly slept last night, replaying the events of the day and grinding over the fact that Sophie hadn't returned her calls or texts. She needed to treat Sophie as a hostile witness at this point and let go of the idea that they were friends at all. "I'll check with Omura and then go over there. I think I can get her to go on the record."

"With what, exactly?"

Lei sighed. "She told me a far-fetched story about her mother being an assassin who wants to kill her. She thinks the poisoned dart was meant for her, and Sari was shot by accident."

Torufu didn't blink. "That sounds about right. Sophie's always been mixed up in crazy crap overseas."

"I know." Lei pinched the web of skin between her thumb and forefinger, a stress-reduction technique Dr. Wilson had suggested. So far it wasn't working. "If what Sophie said is true, we'll get nowhere looking for the assassin who operated the drone; the case is much bigger and more far-reaching than we can deal with on our little island. We need the FBI involved, at minimum." She stared glumly at Torufu. "I was keeping a lid on it for the moment because Sophie swore she was hunting for the perp and would have a better chance of catching them than we would. And I believe her about that, at least."

Torufu scowled. "Let's go see Omura. Right now."

※

Captain C.J. Omura made a steeple of her glossy red fingernails as she eyed Lei from across her immaculate desk. "Tell me again."

Lei glanced over at Torufu. He stared stonily at Lei.

Lei repeated what Sophie had told her. "And then she jogged off and, I believe, got picked up by the Security Solutions private plane to go back to Oahu—or somewhere. She said she was looking for her mother and could find her faster than we would."

"Let me get this straight. You sat on information for a day. Just to—what?"

"Give her time to deliver on her promise."

"And now she's gone off-island."

"It's likely, yes. I'm sorry if I made the wrong call."

"You did. Reach out to Security Solutions and find her. Reach out to the FBI and find her. Get your butt to her house on Oahu and find her. I don't care how you do it. Just freakin' find her!" Omura seldom lost her temper.

"Yes sir." Lei scuttled out and closed the door, leaving Torufu inside. She exhaled as she hurried down the hall. "I'll take that as permission to go to Oahu—right now."

23

Day 7

The jet made a tight circle as it dropped out of the brilliant blue sky to land on the small but well-kept private aircraft runway on Corfu in Greece. As soon as the wheels touched down, Raveaux turned on his phone—and was pleased to pick up a message from Sophie.

The bad news about the drone attack made his belly tighten; but the emotion in Sophie's tone as she bade him take care, as she told him she and the children missed him—that warmed and energized him.

The plane coasted to a stop in front of a stark white stone and plaster arrival building with a red ceramic tile roof. The baggage claim was a long steel counter outside.

"I've already got us rooms in a flat near Pim Wat's address," Raveaux told Rab, who translated to Sam. "I need you to dress to blend with the local population. Wait here in the courtesy lounge while I procure clothing."

Rab nodded. The three checked in through a tiny Customs counter, and Rab and Sam occupied themselves with phones in the small but luxurious private passenger lounge.

Raveaux had dressed carefully before the flight in a white linen shirt and khaki pants with woven leather sandals and a pale straw Panama hat. Hefting his ever-present satchel and sliding on a pair of sunglasses, he blended with other expat businessmen leaving the private airport's arrival building.

He took a taxi to the local market and had the driver wait while he shopped, buying clothing for his two associates and foodstuffs for the upcoming stakeout of Pim Wat's dwelling.

Returning to the airport, he took the clothing back into the building and handed over outfits like his to the men. Rab and Sam didn't take long to change, and Raveaux looked them over critically as the pair came out of the restroom.

"You'll do," he said, adjusting Sam's straw fedora at a rakish angle and showing Rab how to buckle his leather belt so his pants draped properly. "Let's go find our lodging. It's right across the street from Pim Wat's address. Hopefully we can get a surveillance angle from there."

Rab and Sam both preened a bit in their new garb, watching their reflections in windows as they passed; Raveaux suppressed amusement as the trio walked through the exits to the curb, carrying their minimal luggage.

The long-suffering cabbie had waited again, and soon the small, round, bright yellow taxi was rocketing through narrow cobbled streets, headed for the remote coastal town where Pim Wat had made a nest for herself under a new name.

If only Raveaux could cast off his past so easily.

Seated in front with the driver, Raveaux stared out the window, assaulted by memories of a family vacation he and Gita had taken to Santorini Island when Lucie was three.

Gita had loved the architecture of the villages and the folk crafts at the markets. Lucie had loved the clear, warm water and white sand on the beaches.

He had loved his girls' happiness.

Pierre shook his head to dispel the sorrow.

He was here, now, and he had a job to do.

Pastel buildings in characteristic plaster, trimmed in mosaic tile and red clay roofing, clustered along stony streets with pebbled shoulders for walking. Bougainvillea, roses, and geraniums decorated painted doorways with pops of color; lines of laundry flapped between buildings that had been old when Pierre's great-grandparents had been born.

The sun was setting by the time the taxi deposited them at a tall apartment building whose windows were fronted in tiny, ornate mock balconies. One of those, on the fourth floor, would overlook Pim Wat's compound across the street.

Raveaux, unloading a net bag of groceries from the trunk, kept his hat tilted downward to block his face as he gave Pim Wat's property a quick survey.

A high whitewashed stone wall, its top decorated with iron spikes. A solid inset gate with medieval-looking timbers reinforced by black metal strapping with a camera above. An admittance keypad. More cameras over the car entrance.

Nothing further of interest could be seen from the street.

Raveaux paid the cab and followed his companions inside the building.

A tiny but well-appointed lobby was overseen by a man whose neat white beard and dignified bearing matched his surroundings. He didn't speak French or English, and Raveaux knew no Greek, but his healthy wad of cash made sure he didn't have to sign in on the guest book and that nothing about their presence was recorded. Raveaux accepted a large, old-fashioned brass key, and the three men took the stairs to the fourth floor.

Once inside the high-ceilinged rooms, Raveaux dropped his burdens and moved to a tall window that opened over a decorative iron grillwork mock balcony. Standing to the side, he parted the filmy curtains and peered out.

Visibility into Pim Wat's compound was hampered by her high-security wall, and the downward angle of rooflines. Her house was a classic example of older homes of the area: red tile and white stucco over stone, brightened with pots of geraniums at the windows. Built flush against a sea bluff on one side, Pim Wat would have an amazing view of the ocean from the opposite side of the house.

Raveaux knelt and opened his leather satchel, reaching inside for a rifle scope. Applying it to his eye, he scanned the layout of the compound.

Penetration from the ocean might be easiest; sensor lights and surveillance domes were tucked under the eaves of the house from this side.

He backed away and handed the scope to Rab, who took his place. "I'm going to take a quick shower. Get started mapping what you can see of the compound and come up with a plan to get in," he told the ninja.

Rab nodded and spoke a flurry of Thai to his companion. Raveaux took a pad of paper and pencil out of his satchel.

Rab smiled and shook his head. "Scan," he said. Sam had removed a camera with a long lens from one of their gear bags, along with a laptop equipped with a swivel screen. "Photo build map."

"Even better. Good." Raveaux shook his head and stowed his "old school" drawing tools back in his satchel. "See you in a bit."

Raveaux braced his arms on the tiled wall of the shower surround. Under the fall of water, he considered calling Connor.

Pierre had been given marching orders that hadn't been logistically sound, so he'd taken the matter into his own hands without authorization. Hopefully, Mendoza was in the hands of police and off the streets, and they'd found Pim Wat's lair.

But would Connor approve of his course of action?

Probably, now that it had worked.

But the truth was, Raveaux planned to bring Pim Wat in with or without Connor's say-so.

He wanted to be the one to lay that victory at Sophie's feet.

He had no intention of killing Sophie's mother; that would be too hard for Sophie to forget, even if it were forgiven.

Maybe it was hubris, but it would be so satisfying to call Connor after the fact and deliver the news that the mission was complete.

Meanwhile, Sam and Rab were proving their worth. He'd leave

the men surveilling the compound and go out information gathering on his own this evening to see what he could pick up about Pim Wat and her habits around town.

He was in no hurry. The best things in life were worth taking time to do right.

24

Day 8

Sophie was in her exercise clothes, a cup of strong Thai tea in hand, when her father Frank Smithson's resonant voice sounded through the speaker in the kitchen. "Dad to visit Sophie."

"Poppa!" Momi yelled from her highchair. She'd chosen the honorific for her grandfather herself.

Armita smiled at Sophie. "You have time for a visit before that meeting you told me about."

"Indeed, I do, and it's been too long since I've seen Dad." Sophie didn't have to admit her father; his details and face had already been input into the AI security system.

She left Armita with the children in the breakfast nook and stepped out onto the tiled front verandah of the house. Morning in Kailua was filled with the raucous commentary of mynah birds and the soft cooing of turtledoves; a slight breeze rustled the leaves of the mature plumeria tree beside the garage and brought a pink-throated pinwheel blossom spinning to land at Sophie's feet. Waves breaking on the beach made a gentle backbeat lullaby.

Sophie picked up the plumeria and inhaled its sweet, familiar fragrance as Frank's big black Cadillac sedan pulled in and parked in the turnaround in front of the house. Clement stuck his head out of the guesthouse, but Sophie waved him off as she approached the car.

Her father opened the driver's seat door and stepped out. She frowned at how slowly he rose to his feet, as if every joint pained him.

"Dad! What brings you here so early?"

"Do I need an excuse to pop in on my only daughter and grandchildren?" Frank's smile was genuine, though charcoal shadows surrounded his deep brown eyes.

"Armita's got the kids eating breakfast, so come walk with me a minute and see how the new plantings are coming along in front." She wanted an excuse to get him alone. Sophie gestured toward the part of the house where she and a landscaper had carefully designed a framed view of the beach, planted with low native shrubbery easily visible through the high Plexiglas security wall along the front of the property.

"Sounds good. I never need a reason for a walk and talk with my girl." Frank came around the front of the car and embraced Sophie. He held her close for a few long seconds.

She patted his back, feeling the thinness of his once-robust form. "You've lost weight, Dad."

"You've been nagging me long enough to do so," he replied, taking her arm, and turning her toward the pavers that led along the side of the house. "Looks like those vines you planted on the sand out front are really putting down roots."

Sophie frowned but accepted the change of subject for the moment. "Yes, but I'm glad the mature *hala* trees around the lava stone wall were already here." She paused, pointing. "See those two baby coconut palms on either side of the wall? They're cute now, and they'll frame the vista of the beach perfectly when they grow up."

"Nice."

The two reached the front verandah and stared out at the ocean for a moment. "How's work been?" Sophie asked.

"Well, that's part of why I dropped by. I'm officially retired as of yesterday."

"Oh, Dad! Congratulations!" Sophie turned to embrace her father again. "We need to throw a party for you!"

Her father's career as a US Ambassador had been long and colorful; in the years since Sophie had been in Hawaii, he'd been threatening to retire but never had been able to give up the excitement of the work. His last few years had been spent split between Washington, D.C. and working from home at the high-rise apartment in Honolulu where Sophie'd once lived as well.

Frank's mouth tightened. "No party, please. At least not for the moment. Let's sit down."

Sophie braced herself inwardly as they took seats on the glider swing on the beach-facing verandah with its deep roof overhang designed to capture the ocean breezes.

"This retirement date was not my choice." Frank gazed out at the horizon.

Sophie studied his profile, as noble a shape as graced any coin. "You're not well," she stated.

"I'm not." Frank's eyes were bloodshot and haunted when they met hers. "I have stage three leukemia. They say it's treatable; but I'm feeling like a truck hit me every morning, and that will get worse when they start the chemo."

"Oh, no, Dad!" Sophie scooted closer to embrace him, resting her head on Frank's shoulder. Her eyes welled up. "You're my rock, *Pa*. You must get well."

"And I will," he said stoutly. "But I'll be down for a while. Leaving my position of service on a high note seemed the best thing."

"You'll be missed. You should let everyone give you a send-off."

"Perhaps when I'm better. I've got to get through the treatment first."

"You won't be alone. I'll come with you. We'll do it together." Sophie's tears spilled. She sniffed. "I'm ruining your shirt."

"No need for a nice shirt anymore. I'm retired." He rested his head on hers for a long moment.

"I have bad news as well." Sophie straightened up and met Frank's eyes. "Mother has resurfaced. One of her assassin associates tried to take me out using a drone, while I was off island for a case." She filled him in on the attack at the Maui Albatross Sanctuary. "The woman who was beside me and hit accidentally by the dart has died. It's a homicide now. The MPD will be knocking on my door any moment for a statement, at the very least."

Frank's eyes flared wide. "We knew it was only a matter of time until she tried something again," he said darkly. "We have to nail that woman!"

"I verified that she wasn't the one operating the drone. It had to be one of her associates with Mendoza's agency."

"My CIA contact hasn't told me anything about this. Why?"

"I haven't informed them yet. I need to get on that."

They both heard the patter of Momi's footsteps. "Poppa!" the toddler hollered through the French door that opened to the verandah.

"Hold on a minute!" Armita reached and opened the door, Sean in her arms. "Here you go."

"Poppa!" Momi flew across the porch and threw herself onto Frank's lap, hugging him around the waist.

"I'm glad to see you, too, princess." Frank stood and picked Momi up. "Guess what I have in my pockets, Little Bean?"

"Jellybeans?" Momi's smile took up her whole face.

"No, *little* jellybeans!" Frank laughed as the toddler put her tiny hand in his shirt pocket and pulled out several bright Jelly Bellies, holding them up triumphantly. This was their little game, and it never seemed to get old for them.

Frank sat down with Momi in his arms, and she snacked on the usually forbidden sugar treat happily, resting her head on his chest.

Armita carried baby Sean over to his grandpa. "There's someone else who'd like to say hello."

"Hey, little man." Frank gave Sean a tender kiss on the top of his downy head. The baby grinned and waved his arms with his usual good humor; the resemblance he bore to Jake in all but coloring smote Sophie as it often did.

Sophie stood up. "Dad, I hate to cut this visit short, but I've got a morning video meeting in my office. Stay as long as you like—go swimming with the kids. Please don't rush off. The team here is on high alert; Armita will let them know if you do go outside the grounds and they'll keep you covered as far as security goes."

"It's just wrong that you have to live like this," Frank growled.

"Like what?" Momi rifled in his empty shirt pocket. "More jellybeans, Poppa!"

"Only a couple more, or your mama will say I gave you cavities." Frank drew three more beans from the pocket of his trousers. The sight reminded Sophie of Raveaux—her father and Pierre wore the same style of menswear.

How was the hunt for Pim Wat going in Bali? She had to find time to reach out to Pierre and find out.

"Got to go, Dad. Be good, children." She kissed their foreheads. "Armita, I'll check in with you as soon as the meeting's over."

"Take your time," Armita said.

Frank nodded. "I'm going to stay a while. Cool off with this little rascal in the pool," her father said, and Momi whooped with delight.

Sophie slipped through the French door. She was smiling as she headed for her office and the video meeting with Dharma Dawnhorse's young client Bernard Valas, but her expression faded as she walked down the hall.

Her father had cancer. Her fears about his health had been confirmed.

It was treatable. He had great insurance; he'd have the best care. Still, it was stage three, and that was serious. Sophie needed to find out more.

Sophie glanced at the clock; she had fifteen minutes before the video meeting. She used the time to research leukemia and its treatment and prognosis. Much would depend on what type her father had, and he hadn't told her that.

They would walk through whatever came, together.

Sophie grabbed a handful of tissues and let herself have the five-minute crying session that had been so essential in getting through Jake's death. She couldn't afford to slip into depression right now. She had to stay alert and functioning; her family needed her. Her cases needed her.

When the five minutes had passed, according to a *ding!* from her phone timer, Sophie straightened up, dried her eyes, and turned on her monitor for the meeting.

🌴

The laptop tuned into the meeting with Dawnhorse, Leong, and young Bernard "Nard" Valas was set on the corner of Dawnhorse's desk. From her vantage point, Sophie assessed the young man seated in a chair across from Dawnhorse and Leong.

Valas was short, afflicted with acne, and had the kind of bulky build that some men never grew out of. Small brown eyes blinked from behind thick glasses as the boy blew his nose on a tissue; he'd been crying since he walked in and saw that Dawnhorse wasn't alone. They'd got through introductions and the purpose of the meeting as the boy wept; so far, he hadn't spoken a word.

"Our goal is to help you," Sophie said gently. It was important to get Valas talking with something Sophie could spin to a positive. "We have the names of the other two boys involved with the crime, and Ms. Dawnhorse has told us how badly you feel about what happened. If you confirm the other two names and are willing to give us a confession, I feel confident we can get the district attorney to reduce charges against you. How old are you, Bernard?"

"Seventeen." The boy's voice was a hoarse rasp.

"Oh good. Still a minor. Your criminal record can be kept sealed," Sophie said.

The boy cried harder, wrapping his arms around himself, hunching over and rocking.

"I've looked up the other boys involved," Sophie said. "They've both had their eighteenth birthdays. That means they'll be charged as adults."

"He wasn't there. No one can touch him. He made us do it," Valas sobbed.

The boy must be referring to the ringleader, Oz.

"We're recording this meeting, as I first informed you," Char Leong said. "But we'd like you to make a formal statement to the district attorney rather than just telling us what happened. Are you willing to do that?"

Bernard Valas nodded. "Can you make them leave me alone? I just want them to leave me alone."

"That we can do," Sophie said. "I've already contacted Mr. Chang, the District Attorney. I'm going to link him in on this call right now if you're willing to talk to us." She'd tried to reach Marcus Kamuela to join them for the meeting, too, but he was out in the field and not available.

"Yes." The boy gave a single, emphatic nod.

Sophie's fingers flew on her keyboard as she sent the link to District Attorney Chang in his office; moments later, the prosecutor appeared in a window beside her.

"Thank you for doing the right thing, Mr. Valas." DA Chang, though chilly in person, could project sympathy when he chose to. "Have you been informed of your rights?"

The boy shook his head.

Chang quickly recited the Miranda warning. "Do you still choose to go ahead with this confession?"

"Only if you keep me out of it," Valas said, a glint of something in his expression quickly masked by bleary eyes and heavy glasses.

Maybe the boy was playing them, after all.

Chang harrumphed. "I can't promise that. This was a serious crime. What I can promise is that your charges will be reduced to accessory, and your record sealed as a minor."

Valas appeared to think this over. "Can I get it in writing?"

No, the kid wasn't as obtuse as he'd initially appeared.

"I'll fax that over right now," Chang said. "I have a statement prepared."

"Let's wait, then." Bernard was no longer weeping.

Dawnhorse spoke for the first time. "I'd also like you to make a commitment to me that you won't act upon the statements you made to me earlier, about committing suicide."

"I won't have to die if I still have a future," the boy said. "This is the first time I've felt like that might be possible since—that night." Tears welled in his eyes once more. "I'm so sorry. If I could turn back time, I would."

Sophie shifted in her seat as a clerk came in, carrying the faxed document from the District Attorney's office.

Valas signed it. Dawnhorse and Leong also signed it as witnesses.

"I'd like to write out my confession," Valas said. "I don't want to talk about what happened."

"That's fine," Chang said. "But we do need a confirmation of those names right now, and a brief sketch of how things unfolded."

"He said he'd be my friend. That he'd protect me. We'd be the three Musketeers; us against the world," Valas said.

"Who made this promise?" Sophie asked.

"Oz. Remo Ozawa."

"And the other student?"

"Kermit. Neville Ignacio. He goes by Kermit, though."

"So, tell us about that night. Just a sketch."

"Oz said Kermit and I had to prove we were worthy to be in his posse by doing—something way out there no one else would believe." He looked down; his shoulders slumped. "I can't believe it, either."

"Go on," Chang nudged.

"Me and Kermit didn't know what it was. He wouldn't say. Said it was a test, a surprise. We'd go camping on the beach; it would be fun. But he'd packed—the weapons and booze. Stole it from his dad, he said. We hiked out to Ka'ena Point after the park was closed, in the dark. It was kind of cool. We made a fire on the beach; Oz got out the bottle and we drank the whole thing." Valas began to shake; he gripped his knees. "We were drunk when he got out the machete and the tire iron and told us what we had to do. Said it was a test of our strength and loyalty. We went into the fenced area, all three of us—but he stayed outside of the gate. He yelled at us, called us pussies.

Kermit did most of it." The tears had begun to flow again. "When we came out after, we saw that Oz was holding a few eggs. Souvenirs, he called them."

"Where are those eggs now?" Sophie asked.

"He sold them online."

A fillip of triumph zipped up Sophie's spine—she would find that *foul pox-ridden snake* and crucify him; Oz couldn't hide from her online. "Do you know anything about the eggs stolen on Maui?"

"Yes. The kids from Paradise Prep got the idea from Oz. They told us they had an ad out on the darknet. Their eggs are going to someone in China. I heard it was this weekend."

Sophie teased the details out of him—a transfer was going down at the commercial section of the Maui airport in a couple of days. Sophie now had solid information for Lei; maybe that would help her reconcile with her friend.

Chang pulled the interview back on track. "So, at no time did Oz actually injure any birds?"

"No. I told you. He made us do it. Then he threatened us—that he'd turn us in if we talked. He took pictures of us while we were . . ." The boy's voice trailed off. He covered his face with his hands.

Sophie wanted those pictures; they'd show intent, planning, as did bringing the weapons. "Where are the pictures?"

"I don't know. On his phone maybe?"

If they were in cloud storage, Sophie could get them. If they were physically on his phone, Marcus could get them when the boy was arrested—provided he didn't have time to dispose of the device.

"Thank you, Mr. Valas," DA Chang said. "Are you ready to write out your confession now?"

Bernard "Nard" Valas looked up for the first time. "Yes. I'll tell you everything."

Relief was palpable around him. Confession was good for the soul, even if it didn't bring back the dead.

25

Day 8

Lono Jones from Security Solutions met Lei at the baggage claim for Hawaiian Airlines in one of the company's white SUVs.

"Long time no see, Lei." The former detective got out of the vehicle to give her a quick collegial hug and hefted her hastily packed overnight bag into the back seat. "I wondered when our paths would cross again."

"It's been a couple of years, at least, since you left MPD," Lei said, getting into the passenger side of the vehicle. "I was surprised your cell number still worked."

"Well, just because I changed islands doesn't mean I needed to change phone numbers. I figured it must be important for you to reach out and ask for a ride," the lanky blond man said, getting in on his side and starting the vehicle. "Where to?"

"Sophie Smithson's new house in Kailua," Lei said.

Jones slanted Lei a glance from intelligent hazel eyes guarded by thick brows. "I was wondering who they'd send to talk to Sophie about what went down over there."

"You know about the murder at the Albatross Sanctuary, then, and that Sophie is a hostile witness who bailed on the investigation to do her own thing," Lei snapped. "And that I was stupid enough to think she was my friend."

Jones was silent, merging into the busy traffic flowing through the airplane terminal. Lei folded her arms and glared out the windshield.

"There's a lot going on for her," he said at last. "And the danger to her family is real."

"Are you in love with her too?" Lei grumbled. "All the men in her life seem to be."

Jones snorted. "Hardly. Doesn't mean I can't understand where she was coming from in this situation. I also get why you're pissed. But I happen to know a bit more than you do about what's been going on with Sophie's crazy life, and trust me, it's taken a toll. She feels horrible about Sari Gadish."

"She should." Lei softened. "I just want to get an official statement from her, on the record, what she knows about who might have sent that drone."

"She's been expecting someone to come. I know she'll be glad it's you."

Lei didn't reply.

Sophie had a lot to answer for, and the bite of betrayal wouldn't go away easily. It was hard to forget how much she'd lied to Lei by omission, and it had cost the life of a good woman.

"You hungry? It's going on dinnertime, and I haven't had anything since breakfast."

"I could eat," Lei said.

They drove through a burger place for fast food and chomped down burgers and fries in companionable silence as Jones navigated out of the downtown area to drive around Diamond Head toward Kailua.

"You like working private?" Lei asked.

"Sure do. Hours are flexible and nobody's breathing down my neck or trying to take a potshot at me," Jones said. "Pays better too."

"Is that what happened? Someone took a shot at you, that's why you left MPD?" Lei glanced over at her companion. "We were working cases, then next thing I knew, you were gone. I never found out what happened."

"And you won't." Jones flexed his hands on the wheel. "It's nobody's business. I like what I'm doing and where I'm working now."

"Okay, then." Lei got the message. She turned in her seat to look out the window as they followed a curving two-lane road overlooking the ocean around the eroded volcano that was Diamond Head. Off in the distance, a fleet of white boats, some kind of regatta, flew over bright blue seas and caught the sunset in their sails like fast-moving birds. "This reminds me of the Pali on Maui."

"Yep."

Lei remembered that about Jones—the man wasn't chatty.

They entered the enclave of Kailua with its old-money and nouveau-riche homes. Which would Sophie have?

She'd always known Sophie came from money, but her friend—she had to stop thinking of her that way—had never flaunted her background or possessions. What would the beachfront mansion that she'd seemed so proud of be like?

A knot in Lei's chest seemed to loosen as they turned into a driveway lined with mature coconut palms and Lei faced a high lava stone wall consistent with the older homes of the area. The only sign of something new was a featureless black obelisk in front of the high metalwork gate.

Jones rolled down his window and turned his face toward the obelisk. "Lono Jones and Lei Texeira to see Sophie Smithson."

A second went by. They were being scanned.

"Welcome, Lono and Lei." The voice emitted by the scanner was Sophie's.

The gate opened slowly. Jones rolled forward through it up a short driveway into a turnaround in front of a Mediterranean-style villa with a wide, deep porch. A freestanding garage, a miniature of the main building, sheltered beside it in the shade cast by a massive plumeria tree heavy with flowers. Behind, and to the right, stood a similarly styled guest cottage. Two men in black polo shirts and chinos, armed and carrying a bomb detector on a retractable pole, approached.

"Please stay in the vehicle," the older white security agent said. "We need to do a quick vehicle check."

"You got it," said Jones.

The younger Asian man inserted the detector on its pole beneath the SUV, surveying the undercarriage of the vehicle carefully while the older one walked around the SUV and then opened the hatchback and the back door to check the footwells and cargo area. "Step out of the vehicle, please, and surrender any weapons before entering the house," he said.

Lono got out and lifted a pant leg to expose a knife strapped to his calf, which he slid out and handed to the security guy. "Nothing else on me today."

The younger man had finished his check and reached Lei. "Your weapons, please."

Lei held back one panel of her lightweight cotton jacket to show her badge. "I'm a Maui Police Department detective. I don't give up my weapons to anyone."

The young man eyed her, then reached for a radio at his belt. "Ms. Smithson? The detective . . ."

"Sergeant Texeira," Lei growled.

"Sergeant Texeira refuses to surrender her weapons. Shall I deny admittance?"

One of Sophie's exotic curses in Thai filled the air. "Let her in, Clement! She's a friend as well as a police officer!"

"Roger that." Clement remained expressionless as he gestured to Lei. "You may keep your protection."

Lei ground her teeth in annoyance and stomped up onto the covered verandah.

The house, painted a warm ochre with white trim and those weathered pinkish-red roof tiles, managed to look both substantial and welcoming. The tiles on the porch were a deep cobalt blue, a nice contrast.

Lei didn't want to like the place—she was too mad at Sophie.

Sophie opened one side of a pair of large teak front doors. Her dogs, rambunctious yellow lab Ginger and dignified Doberman Anubis, boiled out past Sophie to sniff Lei and Jones as he came up behind her.

The two rascals remembered Lei better than Jones; Ginger hopped up and down on Lei's sneakers, lashing her with a thick tail that shed dog hair all over Lei's black jeans. Lei barely held onto her temper despite Ginger's friendly antics as Sophie approached. She kept her gaze on Sophie's face, noting dark circles under her eyes and the ashy cast of her skin.

"Why did you disappear and leave me holding the bag at the crime scene?" she snapped.

Sophie dropped her gaze. "I'm sorry, Lei. I had to get home and make sure the kids were safe. It was never my intention . . ."

"Never mind your freakin' intention. You left me hanging on a murder investigation you brought down on us, on our department, and the world lost a good person in Sari Gadish. Sorry doesn't fix it."

Sophie shut the front door. "The kids and Armita don't need to hear this. Neither does Lono, for that matter. A little privacy, please."

"Sure. I'll just go in and wait for you two to work things out." Jones stepped through the portal and shut it firmly behind him.

Lei set hands on her hips. Her eyes felt hot. "I thought you were my friend."

Sophie passed Lei and hurried down the steps. "Let's get out of earshot of the AI system. It's recording everything."

That cooled Lei's fire.

She followed Sophie along a series of recessed stone pavers set in the grass to the front of the house and suppressed a gasp at the view of the ocean seen through a high Plexiglas security wall that must be a nightmare to keep clean.

Sophie led her over to a wooden bench under a *hala* tree near the transparent barrier. The wall cut the wind nicely. "We can speak freely here."

"Tell me why you didn't keep me up to speed with what's really going on in your life in the last few years." Lei sat down beside Sophie. "Start talking."

But Sophie didn't say anything; she stared out at the ocean instead. The droop of her mouth spoke louder than words: it spoke of grief, exhaustion, and the depression that always seemed ready to pull her down.

Compassion melted Lei's anger; she'd never been good at holding a grudge against a friend. "It must suck having your mother out to kill you. Mine was a junkie who let me get molested by her boyfriend, but at least she loved me as much as she was capable of."

Sophie's long-lashed eyes, the textured brown of honey, were smoky with pain as she finally glanced at Lei. "I keep waiting for it to stop hurting. I've been waiting my whole life."

Lei reached out an arm and pulled Sophie's much taller, more muscular body over for a hug. "You could have talked to me about all this. I can keep secrets."

"I should have." Sophie's body was stiff; her voice muffled as she pressed her face against Lei's shoulder. "But it's so hard to speak of. A part of me is always wishing and hoping I'd somehow got it wrong, misunderstood my mother's motives. But she's been more than clear. She wants me dead. She plans to take my children."

Lei shut her eyes at the thought of having to find a way to deal with a parent that horrible. "I'm sorry, Soph."

"Me too. And I'm just sick about Sari's death. My mother has a lot to answer for, and I'll make sure she does."

Lei tightened her mouth. "I know you'll do your best, but your mom is harder to kill than a cockroach."

"You are correct." Sophie gave a watery snort of laughter. "But at least I have some good news; we've found the three perpetrators of the Moli Massacre, and I've got some information for you—the name of the kids on Maui who broke into the Albatross Sanctuary and stole live eggs."

"What? Fill me in." Lei took out her phone. "I'll take notes here. We can go inside and record your statement with Jones for MPD later."

"Okay, if that's how you want to do it."

Sophie told Lei how the security officer at the school had tracked down two boys harassing the third perp using a Stingray device, and how that boy had confirmed the names Sophie had matched to phone numbers. District Attorney Chang had been called via video link to join their meeting and had offered the suicidal teen a reduced charge and sealed records if he made a confession; the boy had done so, recorded and witnessed by Char Leong, the school's security officer, and Dharma Dawnhorse, the counselor. At that meeting, he'd also given up the two boys who were planning to sell the live albatross eggs they'd stolen from the sanctuary on Maui.

Lei took down the names of the boys. "I've got to make some calls."

Sophie smiled for the first time. "I thought you might."

Lei stood up and called Torufu on Maui, leaving him a message on his phone with the names of the two students and the fact that the meet to sell the eggs might be coming up. "I'd like to catch them in the act, maybe scoop up the buyer too. We can nip this thing in the bud that way. See you soon, partner." She ended the call and rejoined Sophie on the bench. "What else have you got cooking, *sistah?*"

"My father has cancer. Leukemia. He told me today."

"Oh no." Lei covered her mouth with a hand, her eyes widening. "That's terrible news. How's he doing?"

"He retired, finally. Sad it took this kind of health scare to finally get him to take some time off to spend with his family." Sophie's shoulders hunched miserably. "He's about to begin treatment."

Wayne Texeira, Lei's father, had come back into her life as an adult, after a twenty-year stint in prison. They'd rebuilt their relationship to a firm bond of shared, committed love; the thought of losing Wayne was devastating. Sophie's dad had been her only functional parent. Their rough histories with their moms were a thread that had brought them together as friends. "I'm so sorry, Sophie."

"Yes. Me too." Sophie's smile was a bit wobbly. "Let's go inside and let the babies cheer us up, shall we?"

"Yep. The feel of sticky little fingers on my shirt is a balm to the heart," Lei said. "Can't wait." Sophie chuckled and led the way back toward the front of the house, and Lei used the time following her to plan taking Sophie's statement.

26

Sophie breathed through a wave of apprehension as she opened the big teak front door for Lei to follow her inside. She wasn't looking forward to making her official statement regarding the drone attack. Going on record with her wild story was bound to be awkward.

"Wow, Sophie. Your place is gorgeous." Lei tilted her head to look around the entry, a high-ceilinged area trimmed in antique *koa* wood. "Give me the grand tour."

"Auntie Lei!" Momi came running from the living room to embrace Lei's jeans-clad legs. Soon the three of them, with Lei carrying Momi, did a brief tour of the house, ending with the guest room just adjacent to Sophie's office.

"Has its own bathroom and kitchenette," Sophie said. "This is where you'll stay if I can talk you into an overnight."

"Stay, Auntie," Momi commanded.

Lei laughed, turning in a circle to take in the huge sleigh style bed in *koa* wood with a Hawaiian print quilt with a pineapple pattern on it. "How could I refuse such a great offer? But you need to feed me, too."

"We have food," Momi informed Lei. "Lots."

Both women laughed.

"Where's that baby of yours? I haven't seen him since he was a newborn," Lei said.

"Baby Sean is big now," Momi said. She wriggled to be put down. "I show you!" She ran off.

"Whew," Lei told Sophie. "She's adorable, but you sure have your hands full."

"I know. I truly couldn't manage without Armita." Sophie led Lei back to the living room, where Momi was trying to wrestle Sean out of Lono Jones's capable arms.

"Armita went to get some refreshments, and Momi wanted to carry the baby back to see you," Jones said. "You showed up just in time, I was losing the battle."

"Auntie Lei, here is baby Sean!" Momi gave up the tug-of-war and yelled dramatically, pointing to the baby.

"Yes, there he is—and what a cutie." Lei swooped in to scoop Sean into her arms. "Wow, he's grown, and look at those chipmunk cheeks!" She nuzzled Sean's neck. He giggled—and spat up on Lei's shirt.

"Chaos. That's my life," Sophie said, reaching for a wipe from a box and handing it to her friend. "Sorry about that."

"Glad he saved that little gift for you, Lei," Jones said.

"Oh, he has other gifts to share," Sophie said. "But we catch most of them in his diapers."

Jones, sprawled on the couch, sat forward. "Do I need to be here for your statement?" He aimed his question at Sophie.

"You can go back to the office. I'll take Lei to the airport when we're done."

"Excellent." He stood up with springy grace and tugged his shaggy blond forelock in an imitation of tipping a hat. "Ladies. Many thanks to Armita for the refreshments, though I'll miss them this time. I'll see you around the crime world, Lei."

"Thanks for the ride and the catch-up. Stay out of trouble," Lei said.

"Always." He turned to Sophie. "I'll let myself out—if your AI will okay that."

"She likes you, Jones. In fact, she suggested I input your facial pattern for immediate entry, and I okayed it." Sophie cocked her head with a smile. "Thanks for bringing Lei out here."

"Sure, boss." Jones departed.

Sophie turned to Lei. "Guess we'd better get this over with."

Lei narrowed her eyes. "Sounds like you've got a guilty conscience."

Sophie rubbed the scar on her cheekbone. "If only it were that simple. Let's go get comfortable."

"I'll take the children to the nursery. I poured some beverages for you in the kitchen," Armita said.

"Thanks so much, Armita. I can tell you're the secret to Sophie's success," Lei said. "Do you have a sister that wants to come to Maui and help take care of a very nice five-year-old boy?"

Armita smiled, and it transformed her serious mien. "Unfortunately, no. I am alone in the world. Sophie and her children are my family, now."

Gratitude swelled in Sophie; she acted on affectionate impulses when they came to her, something Momi had taught her—so she hopped up from the couch to embrace Armita. "We are *'ohana*, as they say in Hawaii."

"I like that." Armita squeezed Sophie back. "Now, let's go, children, and leave your mama and Auntie Lei to their police business."

27

Day 8

Connor had rented a vacation accommodation in Kailua on Oahu near Sophie's address, so that he could recover from jet lag and clean up before going to see her. Only Feirn had accompanied him on the long flight from Thailand; though the Master's head of guards had protested loudly, Connor didn't want any more men to accompany him. The bigger their party, the more attention they would draw, and that was the last thing Connor needed.

He was already taking a huge risk by coming and thus violating his agreement with the international task force and the CIA.

But he didn't care. He had to see Sophie and hold her. Comfort her. Make love to her.

The thought of being with her galvanized him like nothing else.

Freshly showered, shaved, fed, and dressed in an unfamiliar western clothing disguise, Connor reached for the straw cowboy hat he'd picked up at a flea market on the way out of Honolulu. Along with the hat, he wore jeans, boots, and a snap front, short-sleeved shirt. A temporary mustache adorned his upper lip; sunglasses obscured his eyes.

"How do I look?" He turned to address Feirn.

The young Thai man gave no answering smile. "We traveled here under false names, Master, and paid for everything in cash. We are wearing disguises." Feirn wore Bermuda shorts, a ball cap, an aloha shirt, and rubber sandals on his feet—a dramatically different look than his usual martial arts garb. "I see how you're trying to keep this travel a secret. Even so, your enemies might be watching." The young man's expression was earnest. Beads of sweat dotted his forehead. "I can't let you go see the Mistress alone. I would be neglecting my duty if I did."

The two of them had left days earlier, taking the compound's helicopter to the Bangkok Airport where Connor, in disguise, had boarded a private jet rented by an offshore shell corporation that had no traceable ties to the Yām Khûmkạn.

They'd had a routine if lengthy flight to Honolulu, where Connor had enjoyed putting on several different disguises and shopping the local markets to get supplies and all he hoped he'd need for his visit. Feirn had been a vigilant companion who blended perfectly with Oahu's polyglot of races; they'd seen no threats and detected no tails so far.

"I appreciate how seriously you take those duties, and that's why you're here with me." Connor made a gesture that encompassed the small but pretty beach house he'd rented. "Do you see anyone else here? No. I trust you to look out for me."

"It's not enough." Feirn lifted his shirt to show washboard abs; tucked into the waistband of his touristy shorts was a nine-mil pistol on one side and on the other, a clip-on holder of throwing knives. "If I'm not there to protect you . . ."

"I'm giving you an order, Feirn. Stay here. The Mistress's house is not far away. I'll text and let you know when I'll be back." Connor whirled on a heel and stalked down wide wooden steps that led to a gravel turnaround where he'd parked his rental, a sporty black Jeep. The open-air model was popular in the Islands, sporting a soft top that could be folded away for an adventurous feeling.

In his current cowboy getup, Connor couldn't look more different than the mysterious Master of the Yām Khûmkạn. But that didn't mean he was safe, neither from his legal enemies nor his illegal ones. Getting hauled in by the authorities would really put a wrinkle in his long-term plans.

"But a long-distance relationship just isn't working for me," he muttered, adjusting his hat as he slid into the boxy Jeep.

Connor pulled out of the driveway and turned right. The two-lane road leading to Sophie's address was narrow but well-maintained, its shoulders lushly planted and neatly mowed. Coconut palms, lush hedges and kamani trees waved their branches and splashed shade on the quiet byway.

So complete was the change of scene that it was hard to believe that until a few days ago, he'd been in his tower prison, plotting his escape. If only he could fling this stupid hat over his shoulder and speed to Sophie while whooping aloud from the heady freedom of being back on his home island—but he was already taking chances, as Feirn had pointed out.

So, Connor watched the speed limit, a ridiculous thirty-five miles an hour, and traveled sedately along the scenic route peppered with mansions until he arrived at Sophie's address.

He drove past it slowly, casing the setup, taking in the high walls, intimidating gate, and security obelisk. She'd described the layout to him on their last phone call.

Should he drive up to the kiosk and announce himself? Getting in any other way would set off alarms and draw attention; yet leaving a trace of himself "on the record" was also foolish and could put Sophie in a bind if she was ever called on to testify as to his whereabouts.

Connor turned around in a neighbor's driveway and drove back, this time pulling up out of visual range of the gate onto the grassy shoulder beside Sophie's rock wall. He took out his phone. As he pressed Sophie's number to call her, Connor heard a roar.

He looked up.

The grille of a large, dark green SUV, much larger and more powerful than his little sport Jeep, was bearing down on him.

28

Once the children had gone to the nursery with Armita, Sophie picked up the icy glasses of passion fruit juice that Armita had poured for her and Lei. She set one down in front of Lei and sat on the white canvas-covered couch near sliding glass doors that opened onto the patio and the fenced-off infinity pool. "Sorry it took so long to get a little privacy. In fact, maybe we should go to my office for the statement."

Lei, dabbing at the blot of spit-up Sean had left on her shoulder, shook her head. "I like it right here, where I can see your zillion-dollar view. And I wouldn't have missed my auntie time with your kids for anything. Now, let's get this over with; I'll ask for only the most necessary information about who might have been taking a shot at you. I'll try not to get into too many backstory questions." Lei took out her phone and thumbed to the Record feature, stating the date, location, and names of people present. "State your name and position, for the record."

Sophie did so.

"Now, tell us where you went after the drone attack."

Sophie outlined the steps she had taken and their direction.

"Why did you undertake to investigate who might have been operating the drone, without authorization or backup?"

"Because I thought the drone attack might have been aimed at me." This was the meat of the issue at hand. Sophie sighed. "My mother, Pim Wat, is a wanted criminal rumored to be a killer for hire. I have reason to believe she has a contract out on my life, as revenge for my participation in turning her over to the CIA some years ago."

"That's why, as soon as the attack was over, you undertook to try to apprehend the drone operator yourself?"

"Yes. In case it was my mother operating the drone. When I verified it was not, I decided to get home as fast as possible to protect my children. She is coming for them, you see." Sophie met Lei's eyes. "She wants to kill me and take my children."

The moment passed as the words settled, forever on the record, burning painfully in Sophie's heart and mind. She drew a deep, shaky breath and sighed it out.

A terrible rending crash of steel outside the gate sounded through the window; both women started as the estate's security alarm went off with a shrill beeping.

Sophie shot to her feet. Lei's hand landed on her weapon as she rose.

Bill's voice came from the intercom on the wall. "Sophie! There's been a serious car accident outside your front gate!"

29

Day 8

Raveaux, Sam and Rab moved through inky dark nighttime water fifty feet offshore from Pim Wat's compound on Corfu. Raveaux wore a supple black wetsuit and fins with a mask and a rebreather device; so did his companions. Their way was lit by small, high-intensity blue underwater handheld lights.

When they reached the approximate coordinates Raveaux had set, he surfaced, lifted his mask, and used a night vision scope to examine the ocean-facing side of Pim Wat's mansion.

Two decks, one on the first floor and one on the second, faced the water. The sliding glass doors were closed, but no drapes were pulled on the downstairs deck which appeared to be separated by a pair of sliding glass doors that opened to a living area. Those unguarded windows revealed that the room was empty and unlit.

His recon in the village the night before had yielded little information on her habits; apparently, she kept to herself while employing live-in staff from elsewhere. Hopefully she was asleep upstairs.

Raveaux scanned carefully for surveillance nodes and spotted one at the corner of each deck level. He indicated them to Sam and Rab, who carried paintball guns with an extra-large paint charge.

The two ninjas shot the surveillance nodes, covering their domes with thick black paint. On the monitoring screens it would seem as though those views had gone dark for some reason, a natural mishap.

The three swam closer, careful not to splash.

The lower deck had stone stairs that led down to the ocean for easy swimming access; but the men approached from one of the sides and scaled the rocks that supported the deck in case there was another camera aimed at the stairs that couldn't be seen.

Once on the house's deck, they lowered waterproof packs and took out their weapons. All three carried high-powered dart rifles loaded with tranquilizers as well as personal handheld weapons.

Raveaux was concerned about other alarm devices. He approached the lower slider and shone an infrared detection device inside, looking for a motion sensor or other detection device. He saw nothing.

He nodded to Rab, who opened a tool kit and extracted a glass cutter. Sam attached a suction cup handle to the area in question as Rab used the cutter. Sam removed a half-circle of glass and Rab reached in and unlocked the door.

The door still refused to open.

Rab peered in through the hole and then gestured to his teammate. Sam removed a flexible metal pole with a hook on one end from his pack, much like a slim jim used to break into cars. He inserted the rod through the break in the glass and hooked the metal bar lying in the door's track which prevented it from opening. With a quick twist Sam lifted the rod up and out of the track and set it quietly aside.

The door slid open.

The three men entered with Raveaux in the lead and their weapons drawn.

Raveaux's pulse thundered in his ears. Sweat broke out over his skin; the wetsuit was designed for warmth in cold water, and he was overheating rapidly in the humid night.

He turned on a narrow-beamed headlamp to light the way. Hopefully their errand wouldn't take long.

Raveaux had been unable to get a floor plan of the house, but the men had crafted a 3D scan of the building's exterior which had enabled a guesstimate of the layout. They crept through the unlit living area; Raveaux kept his attention and senses alert as they navigated the dimly lit space, scarcely registering the shapes of furniture. He turned away from a kitchen, pantry, and office area and entered the wide-open entry, where a set of tiled mosaic stairs led to the second floor.

She would be there, in one of the rooms he could dimly see off the landing. They moved up silently. Raveaux heard nothing but his blood in his ears and his controlled breathing; the ninjas behind him were quiet as black shadows.

At the top of the landing, the three split up and moved to the closed doors of the bedrooms, all of which faced the sea.

Raveaux pressed down on the lever handle of the furthest door and gave the wood of the portal a gentle push; it swung inward noiselessly. He spun around the door jamb and dropped into a shooting stance.

The room was empty and bathed in silver moonlight that poured in through an uncovered window facing the sea; between his headlamp and the moonlight, the room was clearly visible.

On one side, a white toddler bed with storage drawers underneath took up the space; the wall beyond was a pale lavender that translated to gray in the moonbeams.

A chill skittered down Raveaux's spine: this was the same bed and color scheme that decorated Momi's sleeping area at Sophie's new house in Kailua.

He turned to survey the rest of the room, his headlamp tracing a bright beam across the walls.

Opposite the toddler bed was a duplicate of Sean's crib, right down to the type of pacifier the baby used, several piled in a ceramic bowl on a fancifully painted dresser just like the one the children had at home. Even the shelves of books and toys were the same.

This was why Pim Wat had put a spy camera in the children's bedroom, a device Sophie had found and removed—but too late to keep her mother from duplicating the children's quarters.

"Pim Wat's preparing for their arrival," he whispered. Cold sweat rolled down his forehead.

A slight whisper of sound.

Raveaux whirled to face the door, weapon ready; but only Rab and Sam's two faces, caught in the bright beam, blinked at him.

Raveaux lowered his gun. "Where is she?"

"Not here," Rab said flatly. "Gone."

"*Merde!*" Raveaux put away his pistol. "Let's go down to the office and see if we can find some clue as to where she went." A terrible suspicion curdled his gut; what if Pim Wat had left to make a move on Sophie? What if he was too late?

The three men filed down the stairs with no further attempt to disguise the noise of their movements.

Sam and Rab preceded Raveaux into what must be Pim Wat's office, a large room that faced the courtyard and parking area at the front of the house. The walls were lined in closed armoires and ceiling-high shelves were filled with purses, shoes, and hats. Mirrors on stands occupied one corner, and a row of wig stands lined the highest shelf. A desk with a computer on it was placed against the window.

This was more of a dressing room than an office.

Raveaux went to the window and lowered blackout blinds in case of any observation from outside. "I'll go over the computer. You check for a safe, a date book—any trash or receipts or discarded tickets. Let's find out where she went."

The two nodded and went to work, tossing the office with professional efficiency, their headlamps cutting through the dark like the beams of a miner's helmet in the cavelike space.

Raveaux moved behind the desk, a large, heavy antique piece with its back against the windows. He sat down in a cushy leather chair that faced a sleek Mac computer and aimed his headlamp around the immaculate desk—not so much as a pen marred its gleaming expanse.

Whatever Pim Wat did businesswise had to be in this computer.

Raveaux jiggled the mouse to wake it up—nothing happened.

He reached out and touched the power button on the side of the computer, then looked up to see a red digital light flashing on the dome in the center of the room.

He'd just made a grave mistake.

30

The big SUV slammed into the passenger door of the Jeep before Connor had time to do anything but take his foot off the brake.

The phone flew from his hand.

His ears rang with the scream of metal upon impact.

An airbag inflated, engulfing him in blinding white.

The Jeep, absorbing the momentum of the impact, rolled forward, spinning sideways until it hit the thick rock wall that surrounded Sophie's estate and the weight of the much larger SUV crushed it into stopping.

Connor was immobilized by his locked-up seat belt and the inflated airbag.

Breath had blasted out of his lungs. He couldn't see, couldn't breathe.

Slowly, the bag began deflating. Connor sucked in air and pushed the bag away from his face. He mentally scanned his body; though the back half of the Jeep was crushed, the sturdy roll bar over the driver area had protected him; miraculously, he was relatively unhurt.

But someone had pinned the Jeep against Sophie's wall like a butterfly to a corkboard. With the thick rock barrier on one side and the vehicle that had hit the Jeep on the other, Connor was trapped.

Helpless.

They would be coming to finish him off.

He turned as best he could, reaching for the seat belt's fastener, but that seemed to be jammed.

Then, another impact filled the world with screaming metal and shattering glass.

Connor whiplashed in place without the buffer of the deflated airbag, his forehead connecting with the windshield, the back of his skull with the cradle of the headrest.

The scream of rending metal was overwhelming, filling the universe. A smell of burning plastic scorched his nostrils.

The Jeep squashed smaller, its hood compressing and windshield cracking. The Jeep's frame wrapped close, pinning Connor in a steel coffin as effectively as an iron maiden torture device.

Connor bellowed as his legs were compressed. Through flames that burst suddenly out from under the green SUV's mangled hood, he saw Pim Wat's petite blonde silhouette.

🌴

Sophie ran to the door of the nursery with Lei at her heels, the loud beeping of the alarm accompanying them. "Armita! We have a situation outside the gate. I have to check it out."

"I'll keep the children safe." Armita held Sean cuddled close, a hand over his ear to guard against the shrilling noise of the security system. Momi was tucked against her side, a pillow over her head. "Go. See what it is. And turn that thing off before it deafens us all."

Sophie whirled and hurried to the security panel beside the door leading to the garage. She quickly input a code and the sound turned off. "Going to have to adjust that," she told Lei. "This is the first time the system has been activated except to test it. Hopefully it's just a fender bender outside. The men will call nine-one-one."

Ominous-looking smoke billowed from somewhere on the other side of the wall as Sophie and Lei exited the house through the side door and headed for the large front gate which Clement and Bill had opened.

"Didn't you just get done telling me your mama wants to kill you and take your kids?" Lei trotted in Sophie's wake, her weapon drawn. "Maybe you should stay inside with Armita."

Sophie didn't reply, too busy taking in the chaotic scene just outside and to the left of her open gate to answer.

The accident seemed serious. A sporty black Jeep had been smashed into the high rock wall after being hit by a dark green Range Rover; rammed into that SUV, and crushing it up against the Jeep even more, was an older black Cadillac sedan. Sophie gasped—*that Caddy was her father's big boat of a car!*

"Oh no! He must have been coming to visit!" She ran out through the gate, frantic to find him. "Dad!"

Frank stood in the road beside the smoking metal mayhem of the accident, his arms wrapped around a small, thrashing blonde woman, a Glock in one of his fists.

"I know it's you, Pim Wat!" Frank yelled. "Give up. Surrender, and I'll let you live!"

"Never!" Pim Wat screamed.

This was no loving embrace—Sophie's parents were locked in a life-or-death struggle.

Pim Wat fumbled at the waistband of her pants, then stabbed Frank with the knife she'd pulled, hitting him in the side and the thigh.

He released her suddenly, dropping Pim Wat at last—but before Sophie's shocked gaze, he shot her in the head.

The latest incarnation of her mother stared right into Sophie's eyes before falling forward onto her face on the asphalt.

"Dad!" Sophie screamed, running toward Frank as he swayed.

"Help Connor!" Frank dropped his weapon, holding his side. He fell to his knees in the road. "Connor's in the Jeep!"

Sophie spun toward the mass of smoking, crumpled metal that made up the three crashed vehicles.

Fresh flames burst out from under the crumpled hood of the Range Rover. Through the wavering heat, she glimpsed Connor in the front seat of the Jeep. "Oh no! We have to get him out!"

"Holy crap!" Lei exclaimed from behind Sophie. She yelled at the two security men emerging from Sophie's estate, one holding a medical kit and the other a fire ax. "Did you call nine-one-one?"

"On their way!" Bill said.

Lei was right behind Sophie as she ran around the trunk of the Cadillac to the hood of the Jeep. The smaller vehicle was sandwiched between the wall and the nose of the SUV that had hit it. "We need something to get the door open," she said. "But I can't see how. Both doors are blocked."

"Thought this might come in handy." Clement swung the heavy fire ax at the shattered windshield of the Jeep. It folded inward over Connor in a shower of cubelike broken fragments, still connected in one piece. "Get him out through there, before the fire spreads!"

Sophie, with Lei and Bill's help, lifted the broken windshield off Connor and pushed it out of the way. She jumped up onto the hood of the Jeep and reached inside, trying to undo his seat belt. "It's stuck!"

Clement leaped up beside her and swung the ax again, burying its head in the stuffing of the driver's seat and severing the belt. Bill, Sophie, and Lei tugged at Connor's upper body. He was unconscious as they tried to pull him out—but he didn't budge.

"He's trapped," Bill said. "Looks like the dash is wrapped around him. His legs might be crushed."

Sophie wouldn't let herself think about that. She yanked the ax from Clement's hands, jumped inside the Jeep, and swung at the metal wrapped around Connor. Superhuman strength seemed to course through her muscles as she slammed the tool into the crushed hood and door, banging and prying as her friends struggled with Connor's limp body.

Out of nowhere, a young man with a shaved head, wearing an aloha shirt, appeared beside Sophie. He was swinging a heavy metal rod—one of the long, heavy iron spikes that supported the gate. "I'm here to help, Mistress! I'm Connor's personal guard and attendant, Feirn," he yelled in Thai.

Feirn thrust the iron rod into a section of the dashboard that had collapsed around Connor's waist. He leaned back on the makeshift pry bar, groaning with effort. The dash gave way with a squeal, freeing Connor's lower half.

"We got him!" Lei yelled in triumph as they hauled Connor's body out through the broken windshield. "Sophie, get out of there, now!"

Sophie glanced behind her at the hood of the Jeep. Flames had licked to it from the Range Rover. The whole mass could go up any minute. She hesitated, blocked by the fire, but needing to jump out through the opening and across the hood.

Then young Feirn appeared, extending the iron rod to her. "Grab it and I'll pull you out!"

Sophie tossed the ax aside and grabbed the rod. The Thai man hefted her out through the broken windshield with so much strength that they both tumbled off the burning wreck together, landing to roll in the grass.

Sophie scrambled up and hurried to where Lei, Bill and Clement had borne Connor, setting him down on the grass well away from the wreck beside Frank, who'd dragged himself there.

The two men that Sophie loved best in the world lay side by side, in the grass. She glanced down the road; a couple of cars had stopped. Sirens sounded in the distance. "Oh, thank the divine! Help is coming."

Behind her, a sucking *whump!* *Boom!*

The Range Rover and the Jeep exploded into a fireball.

Sophie threw herself over Connor and Frank, instinctively shielding them with her arms and body as bits of the ruined vehicles flew. She squeezed her eyes closed; nothing hit her. "Thank you, sweetie," Frank rasped out.

"Love you, Dad."

Sophie sat up carefully and stared down at unconscious Connor.

Her lover's face was bleached pale. One of his legs appeared broken, his shin twisted unnaturally, blood oozing from numerous wounds on his legs. Cuts from the windshield glass obscured his features and peppered his arms and upper body; a swelling on his forehead distorted his face.

She couldn't tell how injured he really was.

Ignoring the fire going on behind her, Sophie moved over to check on her father.

Frank was still conscious. Lei had found a beach towel somewhere and was pressing it to his bleeding side and leg. "Need to keep the pressure on this wound."

Sophie took her father's hand. "How are you feeling?"

"Like I've been stabbed." The ghost of a smile played around Frank's mouth; his eyes on hers were dark with regret. "I didn't want to kill your mom."

"I know, Dad." Sophie drew Frank's head into her lap and stroked his thick, springy hair with its patches of silver at the temples. "I know."

People were stopping their cars, offering help. Bill waved them off.

Moments later, a couple of police cruisers pulled up; Lei stood and went forward to meet the first responders. She flashed her badge, taking charge of the situation right away and heading off awkward questions and assumptions.

Sophie looked over at Connor; he'd turned his head to the side. His aqua blue eyes were open, clouded with pain, but aware. "I shouldn't be here. No hospital."

Sophie tightened her mouth. "You are absolutely going to the hospital. No telling how many internal or head injuries you have, not to mention a leg that's clearly broken." This man had the power to drive her from the cusp of despair at his possible death to a desire to murder him in mere moments.

Feirn knelt beside Connor on his other side. "The Master must not be seen here. Cannot be recognized," he said.

"But she's dead." Sophie pointed to Pim Wat, lying face down in the road. "The threat is over."

Connor shut his eyes. "I violated the agreement with the task force. They could take me, and they will. They want an excuse."

"I don't believe it. I'm here. My dad is here. We won't let them," Sophie said.

"Frank might not make it. She uses poisons on her blades." Connor's voice was a thread. His body went slack—he passed out.

Frank had begun to shiver; his teeth chattered. "So cold."

"Where's that ambulance?" Sophie yelled toward the officers. Then she addressed her father. "You're in shock, Dad. Blood loss. You'll be fine."

But he didn't seem fine, and a poisoned blade was indeed Pim Wat's trademark. A moment later, he too fainted, his rich brown skin bluish and ashy.

She might lose them both.

"No. I can't bear it," she whispered, stroking Frank's forehead as she held Connor's hand. "Please, God, no."

Feirn set the rod he'd used as a pry bar alongside Connor's leg. He shucked off the aloha shirt he wore and tore it briskly into strips, then wrapped the strips around the bar and leg.

"What are you doing?" Sophie asked in Thai.

"I am stabilizing his leg. I must get the Master to somewhere safe where the authorities can't take him."

Sophie huffed a breath. She'd deal with Connor's ridiculousness later, when Frank was safe.

"Bill, Clement. Help this young man carry my friend Connor into the guesthouse and look after him there. He's refused treatment. We'll deal with his medical situation ourselves for the moment. Hopefully he doesn't have internal injuries."

She glanced over at Lei; her friend was in a huddle with the officers as they put up caution tape and cordoned off Pim Wat's body. None of them were paying attention to her and the two fallen men.

Bill, Clement, and Feirn picked up Connor as carefully as they could and carried him back inside the estate, disappearing from view.

The long-awaited ambulance at last roared up, and its crew surrounded Frank. "This is my father, Ambassador Frank Smithson. Please see that he gets the very best care. He has leukemia but hasn't begun treatment. He's likely been poisoned and needs immediate hydration and a catheter," Sophie said.

"How do you know he might be poisoned?" one of the paramedics asked.

"I have experience with the person who injured him," Sophie said bitterly, staring at the body lying in the road.

The EMTs loaded her father into the ambulance and roared away. She'd follow as soon as she made sure Connor was okay.

Pim Wat was dead.

Why didn't she feel any better?

Yes, Pim Wat was her mother, but that hadn't mattered in a real way for years.

Maybe this odd sense of disbelief was because she had become used to a constant nagging fear of an attack that had finally happened. Removing the threat had left a void.

But still. She needed to see the body up close.

Sophie stood, dusted herself off, and headed over to the crime scene.

31

Pierre Raveaux stared at the flashing red indicator light on a white dome in the middle of the ceiling of Pim Wat's office. The light had turned on the minute he touched the computer's power button. "Alarm activated! We have to get out of here!" he yelled.

Rab and Sam looked up from where they were checking through the costumes hanging in one of the armoires—but before they could move, the dome exploded with a burst of light and a roar.

Their outlines, black against red, were burned onto Raveaux's retinas.

Behind the heavy desk and in front of the windows, Raveaux flew backward, flung by the force of the blast. He barely had time to raise his arms to block his face as he hit the heavy blind; the window behind it broke outward as he was heaved over the sill and out into the courtyard in a shower of flying glass and splintering wood, the desk tumbling over and beyond him. Raveaux landed on the accordion-like blind as the entire window and its covering hit the ground.

All was darkness.

A weight on his chest.

Raveaux dragged in a breath; a million ice picks stabbed his throat and chest. He used his diaphragm to pant shallowly instead.

Darkness filled with floating red spots. He couldn't see.

Pulses of pain, an orchestra just beginning to tune up, jangled along his nerves and reached his brain with an ongoing thump of heavy bass.

A ringing louder than any alarm filled his ears; there was no other sound.

Raveaux curled his fingers; his hands were filled with glass. Shards penetrated as soon as he moved, so he stopped.

His eyelids were stuck shut, or maybe his eyes were gone entirely. There was no way to tell.

But he was alive. That was something.

"Sam. Rab." Forming the words hurt; his lips were lacerated. If he was able to make the sound of their names, he couldn't hear it.

Somewhere close, heat. Increasing heat. A flickering behind his eyelids.

Fire.

She had booby-trapped the house and he'd walked right in and pushed the button that destroyed the place.

And it had killed his men.

Raveaux couldn't suppress a cataclysmic gasp of grief. Tears burst from his eyes. The agony was acute.

A light source beyond turned his vision red.

Muffled sounds came closer, became louder.

Someone wiped his face with a wet cloth and pried one of his stuck eyelids open.

A light filled that eye, piercing all the way into his foggy brain. A voice a thousand miles away asked him something in a foreign tongue.

"Sam. Rab," he tried to say.

They lifted and moved Raveaux onto a gurney.

He thought he screamed at the pain but couldn't hear it.

More wiping at his face; the other eye was freed.

Now he could see the masked faces of medical people above him, and beyond them—flames.

Giant, brilliant flames, reaching up out of the window through which he'd been thrown and clawing up the side of the building to grasp at the roof.

The house was burning.

His men were still inside.

"Rab! Sam!" Raveaux thrashed to get free of the straps they'd anchored his limbs to the gurney with. "Please help! My men are inside!"

But no one listened. No one understood him.

They tightened the straps, ignoring his struggles, and pierced his arm with an IV.

Covered his face with an oxygen mask.

Cranked up the gurney and wheeled him to an ambulance.

Loaded him inside.

"Sam! Rab!" Raveaux sobbed through the knives of pain, trying to communicate, pointing at the house with bloody fingers.

Through the windows at the back of the ambulance, the fire reached up and grabbed for the moonlit sky like the monster it was.

Raveaux shut his eyes and sagged back, sucking oxygen, as the ambulance lurched forward, and the road rumbled beneath it— nothing but pure vibration. The siren on the vehicle was a soft lullaby in his damaged ears.

If only he could go to that dark place where he'd been . . . and stay there, forever.

32

Sophie faced Lei at the yellow crime scene barrier. "I need to see her. I need to say goodbye."

"You can see her from right here." Lei rested a hand gently on Sophie's shoulder. "Getting closer won't change anything."

Sophie studied the woman lying in the road on the other side of the tape.

Pim Wat had landed directly on her face and hadn't moved a millimeter since the shooting. The bullet had entered her temple and exited on the other side; her blonde wig was soaked, forming a blood pool beneath the body. She wore a pretty sundress in patterned, layered silk, and the loose folds, cut like flower petals, fluttered in the wind.

Her feet had fallen so that the toes pointed inward toward each other, an awkward pose she never would have taken in life—but her shoes were distinctive gold Louboutin sandals, identifiable by their red soles.

Good shoes. Expensive shoes.

Pim Wat would have wanted to be wearing good shoes when she died.

Why was it so hard to accept that her mother was dead?

Was she grieving? Or just afraid of a person who could no longer hurt her?

"Okay." Sophie stepped back from the barrier. "I guess that's good enough. I didn't recognize her when she looked at me. She's probably had more work done since the last time I saw pictures of her. She looked like Halle Berry then."

Lei turned to gaze at the body, too. "That's consistent with what you've told me of her *modus operandi*," Lei said. "The Honolulu medical examiner is on her way. I'll mention that you haven't been able to make a one hundred percent visual identification of her as Pim Wat. We'll fast-track a DNA match."

Sophie dropped her head, suddenly exhausted. "Yes, please. I've got to make some phone calls."

"I hope your dad and Connor are okay," Lei said. "After I talk with the homicide detective assigned to your case, I'm going to get a ride to the airport. I might be in time to meet Torufu and intercept the albatross eggs as they're being sold."

"I understand. I really appreciate all you've done."

The two women embraced for a long moment, then Sophie detached gently. "I've got to call the Secret Service and let them know about my father. They can help with the homicide investigation into Pim Wat's death. Must notify the CIA about her death, too."

"Get to it, then, *sistah*," Lei said, giving Sophie a gentle punch to the shoulder. "The worst is over. That witch can't hurt you or your babies ever again."

🌴

Sophie walked inside her compound through the open gate, leaving the chaos of the burnt, destroyed cars and her mother's body behind.

She wasn't ready to go into the guesthouse and talk to her men and see Connor and his new acolyte, Feirn; she was too angry with Connor right now.

Why had he come here? He'd drawn her mother out of hiding

and almost got himself and her father killed! Then, the lunkheaded son of a jackal wouldn't go to the hospital, and now she had to hide him until Pim Wat's death was confirmed.

"*Arrogant son of a yak.* Always thinking rules only apply to other people," she muttered, stalking past the guesthouse. She walked the paving stones to the bench under the *hala* tree, where she'd talked with Lei mere hours before.

She sat down—more like collapsed—and took out her phone. First, she called Kate Smith, her father's loyal Secret Service coordinator. Kate was no longer assigned to his protection detail, since he'd retired, but quickly grasped the repercussions of the situation and confirmed she'd be on the next plane out and would speak to the detective assigned the case on Frank's behalf.

Next, Sophie called CIA agent Devin McDonald. "My mother's dead," she said flatly. "Shot outside my compound by my father, Frank Smithson. He's been stabbed—likely poisoned. I just wanted to let you know so that, if you hear of Connor traveling outside of Thailand, his bargain with you is fulfilled."

"Good news about Pim Wat, though I'd have liked another crack at interrogating her," the man said. "And how is his bargain fulfilled, if your father killed Pim Wat? Connor was supposed to bring her in."

Rage blurred Sophie's vision.

She was trapped; she couldn't tell McDonald how Connor had paid in blood to lure Pim Wat into the open, without revealing that he'd also violated his immunity agreement.

Connor's instinct to hide from the CIA was justified.

"*You low-down dirty gutter rat with pustulant hemorrhoids*," she snarled.

"Ah. The famous Sophie curses. I understand Thai, you know."

"Then you understand how much I despise you and hope you fry in hell and make a juicy feast for the demons, fat pig that you are."

"Tell me how you really feel, Sophie." McDonald's rich chuckle showed that he enjoyed the upper hand. "And tell your boyfriend in Thailand I still have work for him to do—overseas, where he belongs. I'll send a contact from our office in Honolulu to confirm Pim Wat's death."

He hung up.

Sophie dropped her phone onto the bench beside her and covered her face with her hands. She was too weary to even stand right now; the aftermath of adrenaline overload had hit her hard.

Connor would be fine at the guesthouse a little longer; her father was in the best possible hands. She'd attend to them later.

Right now, she needed to see her children and update Armita. She'd kiss her babies' cheeks, know they were safe, and enjoy as they hugged her, too.

Momi and Sean gave her strength.

Sophie hurried up the steps and entered the house through the big slider on the ocean-facing front verandah.

"Armita?" Her voice rang hollowly as she walked through the living room; no one answered.

Maybe Armita had barricaded the three of them into the nursery; that made sense.

Sophie hurried down the hall to the children's room and yanked open the door.

The nursery was empty.

"Armita! Momi! Sean!" Sophie shouted now, whirling around, terrified. Her voice bounced back at her from the bare walls of the hallway. She gripped the doorframe, sucking in a few breaths to calm herself.

This was a smart house. The AI would know where they were.

"Angel. Where are Armita and the children?"

"Armita and the children are in the safe room." As always, Angel's voice was Sophie's, and that was a bit weird, but she sighed in relief anyway. Armita must have heard the gunshot and taken the kids to the basement.

Sophie hurried to the kitchen—and drew up short at signs of a struggle.

Chairs tipped over.

The knife block had spilled blades all over the central counter island.

A jar of spaghetti sauce was broken against the wall, spilling red liquid as thick as blood all over the floor.

Under the table was Armita's phone.

Sophie rushed over to pick it up. An incomplete call to her own number showed on the screen.

"Angel. Are Armita and the children safe?"

"Yes. Armita and the children are safe." Angel's voice was maddeningly calm and deliberate.

"Is anyone injured?" Sophie was already at the pantry where the automatic elevator that led down into the safe room was hidden.

"Armita is injured."

"The children?"

"The children are not injured."

Sophie fumbled with her phone, calling Lei even as she opened the panel to get behind the rack of canned goods and get in the claustrophobically small dumbwaiter that led directly to the basement panic room. "Lei, there was an attack here in the house. Armita is in the basement with the kids and the AI says she's injured. Whoever it was must have run away. Can you have the officers do a sweep, and alert my men? I need to get to Armita and the kids and find out what's going on."

"On it," Lei said.

Sophie ended the call and got in the elevator.

It closed, and began descending at its usual slow, steady rate. Sophie shut her eyes, breathing deliberately—in through the nose, out through the mouth.

Armita was injured, but the children were not.

The AI had not called her phone as it had been programmed to do in an emergency. Why hadn't she been alerted, or Clement and Bill? Something was wrong with the system. "Great time to find out Angel's broken," Sophie muttered.

The elevator opened.

Sophie clapped a hand over her mouth to keep from crying out in shock.

The children were fine.

Sean was sleeping in his carrier, and Momi was sitting inside a fenced play area, fully occupied with several plastic tubs of brightly colored, soft clay.

Armita sat with her back to the fence containing Momi, her body angled to conceal the small pistol she held pointed at a woman, gagged with one of Sean's bibs, whose hands were bound to a low overhead pipe: a petite, tawny-skinned woman with fashionable long brown hair and heavily made-up eyes: a woman Sophie recognized. "Mother."

Pim Wat blinked dramatically long false eyelashes once, in acknowledgement. Her eyes were an unnatural green.

Sophie went straight over to Armita. "Angel said you were hurt," she hissed, trying not to draw Momi's attention.

"Just a scratch." Armita lifted the arm tucked against her side. Blood on her ribs stained her black shirt darker. "Not poisoned. I got her blade away; she nicked me with one from our butcher block."

Sophie whirled to glare at her mother. Pim Wat shrugged.

"Mama!" Momi had spotted Sophie and jumped up from her play.

"Hey, Little Bean." Sophie crouched to hug the toddler for a long, fervent moment. "Let's go back upstairs, shall we?"

"Yeah! It's stinky down here." Momi wrinkled her nose. The room smelled like the strong perfume Pim Wat wore.

Sophie picked up Sean's carrier, bending to kiss his sweet forehead. "Are you able to walk, Armita?"

"Of course." Armita pushed herself upright with the hand not holding the gun. "But I should keep an eye on this one." She gestured to Pim Wat with the barrel.

"No. I have a better idea." Sophie bared her teeth in a smile. "We'll just turn off the lights when we leave. You know how dark it gets down here when that happens. She won't be going anywhere."

"Who that mean lady, Mama?" Momi took Sophie's hand, staring at Pim Wat with troubled eyes. She popped a finger in her mouth. "She tried to hurt 'Mita."

"Nobody important, darling." Sophie shepherded Armita and the kids ahead of her to the elevator. "You get on up with the children. I've alerted Lei and the police that we'd had an intruder, so they'll be looking for you. I'll turn off the lights and come up in a moment. Say nothing to Lei about what happened."

"All right." Armita gazed at Sophie intently as she got on the elevator, holding Sean's carrier with her good hand, Momi tucked behind her. "Don't take Pim Wat's gag off, Sophie. You don't need her poisoning you with her lies."

"You're right, as always. I can't wait to hear how you got the best of her. I'll be right behind you, I promise." Sophie blew a kiss to Armita and her children as the elevator closed on them.

She turned back to face her mother. "You came for me, first, after all."

Pim Wat blinked a yes and made a gesture for Sophie to remove her gag.

"No. Armita's right. You don't get to speak to me. But I've got a few things to say to you."

Sophie moved closer. She put her hands on her hips and stared down at the woman who'd given birth to her, now her worst enemy. "I am going to leave and turn off the lights. When I go upstairs, I'll tell Lei and the cops all is well and that the intruder must have run away. And then, I'll put my children to bed and go to the hospital and sit by my father's bedside. If he dies . . ." Sophie pointed at her mother. "If he dies, I won't come down here again for . . . oh, two weeks ought to do it."

Pim Wat's eyes widened. Her hands came together in an imploring gesture. She blinked rapidly and tears filled her eyes, overflowing to leave mascara tracks on her cheeks.

"You're a great actress, Mother, but I'm not fooled. I don't know who your partner was, dressed up to look like you, but she stabbed Dad, and then he shot her. All very Shakespearean, and right outside my gate." Sophie shook her head, musing. "But something was off.

Something about her, much as she looked like you—she wasn't you, and some part of me knew it." Sophie came closer, close enough to smell the stink of fear overpowering Pim Wat's cologne. "If Dad lives, I may call Agent McDonald in time for him to come get you before you die, and then you can go back to your favorite place—Guantánamo Bay. McDonald's very eager to see you again. One might even say he's obsessed." Sophie leaned over and checked the knots that bound Pim Wat, tightening them. "Enjoy the dark. I learned to love it with Assan Ang, who you gave me to. There's a special craziness that comes when you never see any light. For days."

Pim Wat lashed out with a foot, but Sophie easily sidestepped. She shook a finger at Pim Wat. "You know, I was considering tying you so you could sit down. But now . . . no. You can stand there until your legs give out. And then your arms. Eventually, your bladder and bowels."

Pim Wat shook her head vigorously, making pleading noises through the gag.

Sophie turned and walked back to the elevator. She stepped inside the dimly lit steel box. "Goodbye, Mother."

She reached outside the door and shut off the light.

The darkness was absolute.

The door closed on Pim Wat's frantic, begging moans. Sophie savored the sounds as the elevator carried her up, and into the light.

33

Day 9

Raveaux woke, and in a few moments, his senses booted up and sent him information.

Smells of cleaning solvents, iodine, urine.

Sounds of muffled voices, clanking, a beeping somewhere. Hearing was still bad. Maybe his eardrums had been blown.

Dry, metallic taste in his mouth.

Breathing still hurt. His hands hurt.

Merde, everything hurt.

Raveaux pried his eyes open; they hurt, too, but those eyes would tell him the most about where he was and what had happened.

He was in a hospital bed. His ribs were strapped, and so were his hands and arms. An IV ran into one of his hands, and on the other was a handcuff attached to the bed.

He shook the handcuff in dismay. It must have clattered loudly enough to attract attention because a nurse appeared.

She spoke in a flurry of indecipherable words that barely penetrated the cotton wool in his ears. He gestured to his head with his free hand. "I can't hear. What's wrong?"

He said it in English, then French. She frowned, shook her head, poking and checking a bandage around his head that should not have caused the hearing problem. After checking his assorted hookups, she disappeared.

Raveaux peered at the window; it was covered with a heavy metal mesh. This had to be a secure medical facility.

"*Bonjour.*" The doctor at his bedside held a clipboard and was speaking loudly enough in French for him to understand. "What is your name, *Monsieur?* You had no identification with you when you were brought in."

"My ears." He gestured. "What's wrong with them?"

"One of your eardrums was burst by the blast, and the other sustained damage. You should recover in time." The man had a thin nose and heavy glasses that kept sliding down; he pushed them back up as he read Raveaux's chart. "Broken ribs. A bruised spleen and liver. Concussion. Multiple lacerations from glass." He folded down the paper he was consulting and eyed Raveaux. "You are very lucky, for a terrorist."

"Terrorist! Hell no. I did not set that bomb," Raveaux exclaimed. "I was just—did they bring anyone else in with me? Anyone else injured in the explosion?"

"No. And I'm only a doctor; I am not the one you must explain yourself to. I just know what I was told. Now that you're awake, I'm sure someone will be arriving soon to interview you." The man hung his chart on the foot of the bed. "Try to rest. That is what you need to heal."

"Please. I must make a phone call." Raveaux lifted his hands, trapped by the cuff, in a pleading gesture. "I promise I'm not a terrorist. I'm a former policeman, an investigator. That house was booby-trapped by someone you really don't want in your country. Please, I'm begging you. Just a phone call? Surely, I'm entitled to that."

The doctor glanced at the door; clearly his conscience was struggling with his bias.

He reached into his white lab coat and took out a cell phone. He unlocked it and handed it to Raveaux. "I am listening to everything you're saying."

"Of course." Raveaux's hand trembled as he took the phone; his fingers were thick with bandages and clumsy as he swiped at the screen. "I can't . . ."

The doctor rolled his eyes and took the phone back. "Tell me the number."

Sophie's number was the only one Raveaux could remember in the moment of stress. He told the doctor the digits; the man pressed them and handed the phone back.

Raveaux held it to his damaged ear. Way off in the distance he could hear ringing, then Sophie's voicemail, her voice muffled.

Disappointment was crushing.

"Sophie. I'm in Corfu, Greece, in a secure hospital. The mission went bad. The house was booby-trapped, and my men are dead. Please send help; they think I am a terrorist and I'm being held here." He paused. "She wasn't there. Be careful, she might be coming your way."

He ended the call and handed the phone back to the doctor. The man slipped the phone into his pocket just as a plainclothes detective and a uniformed officer pushed through the door.

Raveaux shut his eyes and went limp, feigning unconsciousness.

Maybe he could buy a little more time for Sophie to send someone, before he ended up in a Greek jail—permanently.

Pim Wat's eyes burned where the last bit of light had been extinguished with the closing of the elevator door; the rectangular shape of it echoed in her vision, red and pulsing, as her eyes strained in vain to find anything to fasten upon.

Time had ceased to matter, to have any meaning, except in the varied layers of agony she experienced as her body begged for the relief of being able to sit or lie down or relieve itself.

Her mind played the scene that had led to this moment in a feedback loop of reproach.

All had been going according to plan. Her source at the Yām

Khûmkạn had tracked Connor's departure for Hawaii. The assassin she'd been working with had made an attempt on Sophie using a drone; she'd cursed long and loud when that went awry. Sophie would be on alert, and so would the authorities. Time was of the essence. It had seemed fortuitous when Connor went to visit Sophie; Pim Wat could eliminate her targets in one fell swoop. The assassin double she'd worked with through Mendoza had been game for a trip to Hawaii and they'd made their move, tracking Connor to the estate.

While the double used the rental SUV to take him out, Pim Wat had slipped in the open gate and into the house, whose alarm was deactivated as she'd hoped.

She'd entered via the side door—only to encounter Armita in the kitchen, preparing a bottle for Sean; the children were not in sight so they must have been in the nursery.

"Pim Wat," Armita had said, with surprise on her plain face. "I might have known."

"You recognize me? Well, you haven't changed a bit, Armita. Ugly as ever."

She should've silenced Armita then and there, but she'd wanted to terrorize her a bit first. The woman had been her handmaid for almost twenty years; Armita's abandonment and betrayal had hurt Pim Wat more than Sophie's ever had.

Armita wasn't scared, though. She grabbed a chopper out of the block and threw it at Pim Wat, who'd barely managed to dodge it.

"If that's how you want it . . ." Pim Wat pulled her favorite knife and leaped for the wiry little woman to finish her off.

Armita surprised her again; she knocked the poisoned blade out of Pim Wat's hand and dove for the doorway. Pim Wat grabbed a butcher knife from the fallen block and threw it, slicing along Armita's ribs.

But her former maid wasn't trying to escape, she'd been aiming for the pantry. Armita grabbed a jar of Italian sauce and threw it, and that was the last thing Pim Wat remembered.

She'd woken up here, hanging from a pipe in the ceiling of the basement, gagged with one of Sean's bibs.

Humiliating as hell.

Enrique Mendoza had offered Pim Wat a cyanide capsule during one of their meetings at the Paris office. "It's a microdose mixed with sleeping medication. None of that ugly frothing at the mouth or seizures like the old days. You'll nod off like falling asleep, and then . . ." he snapped his fingers . . . "your heart will shut off."

Pim Wat remembered the day so distinctly; the Paris light, clear and almost silvery in hue, had come through the window to caress Mendoza's coiffed head, falling over her hands in their little lace gloves like a caress.

Talk of death had seemed foul. A blight. Ridiculous.

She was Pim Wat; she had more lives than a cat. If she was ever taken, she'd survive to escape another day.

"No, thank you," she'd said. "I always find a way."

"I believe you. Just thought I'd offer." He'd returned the capsule in its plastic bubble pack to a bottle with several others. "It's a perk I offer all our operatives. You never know when such a course might become a way out that makes sense."

If she'd had that capsule with her . . . Pim Wat was glad she didn't have that temptation because right now, an easy death was appealing as darkness pressed in on her, unforgiving and absolute.

Her legs ached; her throat was sore from trying to communicate, her mouth raw, her bladder full. Her heart hurt from Sophie and Armita's ruthlessness; she hadn't believed those two had the stones to do this to her.

And things were going to get worse before there was even a chance they might get better.

Frank would live, because the man was that stubborn, but mostly because it wasn't likely that her double had used poison on her blade.

That left Pim Wat standing here in the dark, waiting for the CIA. There was no way that fat, vindictive fool McDonald would let anyone else pick her up; that meant she probably had to endure two days without food, water, or a way to rest before he came.

Pim Wat hung her head in exhaustion. She loosened her knees, so she hung from her wrists, taking weight off her legs for a few moments. She moaned in self-pity.

But she couldn't afford the lost water of tears, and after a bit she stood back up and mentally marshaled her resources.

She would go deep inside to that place where nothing and no one could reach her. She'd stayed in that gray inner place for two years the last time they took her to Guantánamo Bay.

When they came this time, she'd be ready, and she'd make them pay before they took her there again.

34

Connor came to awareness, hearing male voices talking over his head. "Low blood pressure. May have internal injuries," an older voice said. "We can't be responsible for this."

"We're just following orders. Keeping him here for a little while," a younger one replied.

Connor kept his eyes shut as he tried to assess the situation: was he with friends, or foes?

"I'm here with you, Master." Feirn whispered in Thai in Connor's ear. "You're hidden. Safe inside Sophie's compound. We've bought some time."

"Hey! What are you saying to him?" The older voice sounded concerned.

"No English," Feirn said.

"Who is this guy, anyway?" Older grumbled.

"He seemed to know the blond guy. Maybe they're together," Younger said.

"Weird shit going on," Older said. "The cops should be in here, taking statements."

"Sophie's friends with the cops, and she said wait. So, we wait," Younger said. The two moved off into another room, still arguing.

Feirn's breath was warm on Connor's chilled cheek. "Master. You have some time alone now. Concentrate. Go inside and heal yourself. I know you can do it. I've seen you do it."

Feirn was right. Healing himself was the best use of Connor's limited resources right now; if he could mitigate his injuries, maybe Sophie's two men wouldn't insist he go to the hospital.

But without the warm, womblike waters of the Yām Khûmkạn fortress's healing baths, it was hard to concentrate.

His broken leg throbbed with every beat of his heart, his brain felt too big for his skull, a million glass cuts cried out for attention, and his neck was a bundle of live nerves, lighting up his spinal column with flashes of electric agony every time he moved.

Whiplash was no joke, but none of his injuries were life-threatening.

"You can do this, Master. Concentrate. Leave the leg for last," Feirn said.

Connor groped for the young man's hand, then squeezed it. "Thank you for disobeying me, Feirn, and being there when I needed you," he whispered.

"It's my pleasure to serve you, Master." Feirn said. "Now focus. Send energy where it needs to go to heal your body."

Connor kept hold of Feirn's hand, and concentrated.

Deep inside his body were conduits of blood, the pump of his heart, elaborate cables of nerves, the intricate processing plant of his organs, all built upon a sturdy structure of calcium bones.

Connor visualized the rich indigo of his energy field moving along liquid pathways with his heartbeat, repairing the many damages as Feirn kept up a steady whisper of encouragement in his ear. Gradually, the insistent jangle of pain receded.

His mind grew clearer as the electric zaps of nerve pain stopped.

His leg was still a wreck, but he'd at least silenced the loud throb of it. He squeezed Feirn's hand again. "Thank you. I will rest now and do more later."

"Water, Master." Feirn slid an arm under his head and neck to lift him and held a glass to his lips. Connor drank thirstily, then drifted off into sleep.

He woke to the sound of Sophie arguing with the men in the adjacent room. Feirn was nowhere to be seen. "It's not your responsibility to decide what happens with Connor's injuries. What you need to do right now is fix Angel. The alarm should have gone off again when an intruder got into the kitchen and attacked Armita! Angel should have called our cell phones, whether I'd manually deactivated her or not!"

Connor's pulse jacked. His eyes flew open. *What had happened?*

He needed more information. Needed to understand what was going on so he could figure out a strategy, how he could help.

"Thankfully, Armita drove off the intruder and got the kids down to the panic room. They're okay, no thanks to you!" Sophie was really ripping into her security detail.

"Sorry, Sophie. Won't happen again," Younger Man said.

"I keep hearing that, but it's not good enough. Now, stop second-guessing me and figure out a way to move my boyfriend. I want you to bring him over to the guest room in the main house."

"Right away, Sophie," Older Voice murmured, chastened.

"We can put him on the foldable cot bed and carry him that way," Younger said.

She had called Connor *her boyfriend.*

He shut his eyes and smiled. He didn't need to figure out a strategy or a way to help; Sophie was handling things just fine.

Their footsteps approached. Even with his eyes closed, Connor could see three energy signatures against the red of his closed lids. Sophie's aura was a brilliant, pulsing purple; the men were mere shadows beside her.

"Sophie." He smiled up at her. "You're a sight for sore eyes. Literally."

"Connor." Sophie's gaze was potent, taking in every detail of his face. "You're looking much better." She leaned down and kissed him, a harsh stamp of ownership, in full view of the men.

His whole being lit up.

Yes, she was angry at him—likely for coming here and getting hurt—but she was glad he was there, nonetheless.

"Clement, Bill—get Connor on that cot and over to the house. Make up a bed for Feirn, too. Make sure they have everything they need for comfort, and then get to work on the Angel problem. I'm going to the hospital."

Connor caught her wrist. Her pulse pounded under his fingers. "What's wrong? What happened?"

"My father was stabbed by a—by Pim Wat. He's in bad shape."

She wasn't telling the full truth. He stared into her eyes. "Tell me."

"Later. Send all the prayers you can to my dad that he survives." Sophie tugged out of his grip. "This whole thing is your fault, *son of a goatherd!* What the hell were you thinking, coming here?"

Connor cut his eyes over to their audience. "As you said. Later."

"I'll see you when my father is dead or out of danger, then, you *idiot horse's behind.*" Sophie whirled and stomped away.

"I love you too," Connor called, but she was already gone, the door banging behind her.

Clement and Bill, with Feirn's help, transferred Connor onto a folding cot and then used it as a stretcher to carry him inside Sophie's mansion of a house. Connor propped himself up on his elbows, staring around at the place. As they passed through the living room, Connor spotted Armita with the children. She lifted a hand to wave, and Momi caught sight of him.

"Unco Connor!" She flew across the room, then came up short, intimidated by his wounds. "Are you hurt, Unco?"

"Yeah, Little Bean, but I'll be okay. Come visit me when I'm all set up in my room," he said, and the men carried him on.

The guest room was huge, with a king-sized bed and a fold-out couch for Feirn to use that Clement said he'd bring sheets in for. A giant whirlpool bathtub and small kitchenette behind folding doors completed maximum comfort and functionality.

Once Bill and Clement had set them up, the two departed, presumably to work on "the Angel problem."

"Can you bring Armita in?" Connor asked. "The nanny. I need to speak to her and find out what's been going on. She speaks Thai . . ."

"Yes, Master." Feirn ducked his head and hurried out.

Connor looked around the room, taking in the neutral but warm buff wall color and Hawaiian print drapes paired with vintage rattan furniture. Sophie had updated the house but kept the feeling of its original era and struck a nice balance in doing so.

Armita came in, carrying Sean in one arm. The other was strapped to her side with a sling. Momi ran over to give Connor a hug. "Are you ok, Unco?"

"I am." Connor smiled; the cuts on his face and arms already felt itchy with healing, though dried blood probably made it look bad. The leg gave a painful pulse as he moved; something would have to be done about setting that, though. "I've missed you, Little Bean."

"Missed you too." She rested her silky head on his shoulder for a moment. His chest hurt with love. He patted her back.

Armita introduced Momi to Feirn and told her to fetch her block set to play with while the grownups talked. Momi ran off with Feirn in tow.

"Can I hold him?" Connor asked, reaching out an arm for Sean.

"No. You're injured." Armita took the armchair near the bed and settled the baby on her lap. "You can see him from here."

Connor gazed at the baby. Sean was radiant with health and good energy; his changeable hazel eyes tracked every move Connor made as he cooed and babbled. "He's beautiful. Reminds me of Jake." He frowned at Armita. "What happened in the house?"

"Pim Wat. She came for the children while Sophie was occupied outside—with you."

Shock widened Connor's eyes. "But I saw her . . ."

"You saw an assassin who dressed up as Pim Wat used to look. One of Mendoza's people."

"How . . ."

"Pim Wat sneaked in during the distraction at the gate. She came at me in the kitchen with her knife. I knocked it away. She grabbed another knife from the block and threw it at me. Gave me a scratch on the ribs. Then, I nailed her with a jar of spaghetti sauce." A wicked gleam lit Armita's dark eyes. "Unfortunately, she lived."

Connor shuddered in reaction. "Where were the children?"

"They were in the nursery, thankfully."

"They could have been hurt!"

"She did not want that. I did not want that. So, no. They wouldn't have been hurt." Armita's certainty was bracing.

"And then?"

"She went down. I tied and gagged her and took her to the basement. Then, I went back up and got the children and brought them down too. We waited for Sophie to come. And she did."

"And Pim Wat?"

"Still in the basement. And yes, she's alive." Armita paused thoughtfully. "Unless Sophie killed her when I left them alone together. But I don't think so. She told me she'd leave her in the dark for McDonald to fetch, and then play with."

Momi returned. Feirn followed, carrying a bin of blocks. "You want to play, Unco Connor?"

"Thanks, Little Bean, but I need to rest right now."

Armita fetched a bottle of formula and fed Sean. Both seemed unperturbed by the events of the day. Connor watched Momi and Feirn stack blocks on the floor, his mind in a whirl.

Somewhere beneath them, Pim Wat waited in the dark.

Alive.

35

The smell of burning plastic, hot metal and spent fuel assaulted Sophie's nose as she headed for her car after seeing to Connor's transport to the main house. She glanced at the open gate; she was on her way to see her father in the hospital, and there was no point closing the entry when the threat was over.

"Why shut the barn door when the horse has galloped away?" she muttered.

Her phone toned with an incoming call; Sophie stopped to look at it as a voicemail from an unknown number registered. She didn't have time to listen to a strange message now. She'd pick it up once she got on the road for the hospital.

She slid the phone back into her pocket as Lei approached.

"Going to see your dad?"

"Yes." Sophie paused; she'd told Lei and the other first responders when she came up from the panic room that the intruder had run off. She hated to lie, but couldn't risk Pim Wat becoming entangled in the investigation and being taken away; she needed her mother as a bargaining chip with the CIA. "I've got to see how Dad's doing."

"I just called the hospital for an update. Good news: they say he's holding on."

"Thank you." Sophie embraced Lei. "That will keep me going until I get there and can verify his status myself."

"Well, it's been real, and it hasn't been fun," Lei quipped. "I've got to go to the downtown station; they want me to make a statement there, then promised me a ride back to the airport afterward."

"Then it's goodbye for now." Sophie's brows drew together. "We really didn't get to visit."

"Yeah. I'd hang out longer, but I want to be with Torufu when he busts those egg sellers at their meet on Maui, and it's coming up soon."

"Of course. Thanks for everything."

The women embraced. Lei waved as she jogged away toward the open entry, her slim figure and bouncing curls giving an impression of youth and energy that belied her thirty-something age.

Sophie was lucky Lei had forgiven her for withholding information about the drone attack. After all this was over, Sophie'd tell her about capturing Pim Wat, too. Hopefully, Lei would understand the bind Sophie had been in. "It's easier to ask forgiveness than permission," their mutual friend Marcella's voice said in Sophie's mind.

Sophie opened the side door of the garage and got into the SUV. After the last intense hour she'd spent dealing with the accident and the attack that had ended up with her mother in the basement, the familiar surroundings of her car felt like a sanctuary.

Something was nagging at her—something unfinished. What had she forgotten?

Sophie grasped the wheel and concentrated on the nagging sense of something important missing. The persistent feeling had been going on for days . . . what was it?

Pierre. Pierre Raveaux. He was missing.

Her calm rock in a storm was gone, and she didn't know where.

Maybe he'd called from an unknown number, and she hadn't yet listened to the message?

Sophie fumbled the phone out of her pocket and punched the voicemail app, listening.

Pierre was in Greece. An explosion at Pim Wat's house. In the hospital, arrested as a terrorist... and his men were dead.

"That poxy whore!" Her hand tightened involuntarily on the phone, her heart thundering as the message ended. "Poor Pierre!"

What could she do for him so far away?

There was only one person in the world who could help, and she had to call the nasty son of a snake anyway.

As soon as Sophie had driven out through the open gate, past the smoking wreck of the accident now mobbed with cops, and the crime scene which had been cleaned up to make way for traffic, Sophie called Devin McDonald at the CIA.

"Agent McDonald. I have news. Connor has taken Pim Wat captive." The lie was necessary for Connor's contract to be fulfilled; Armita wouldn't mind this bending of the truth. At least, Sophie hoped not; she'd discuss it with her later. McDonald was too arrogant to interview local law enforcement about what had really happened and find out anything different.

"Well now." The fat man's voice was rich with sarcasm. "How did she go from dead at the hands of your father a few hours ago to taken into custody by Connor, now?"

"The woman my father fought with was a decoy. Probably one of Mendoza's assassins. She was likely supposed to take me out, but my father intercepted her. While we were all occupied with that situation, which involved cars outside my front gate, the real Pim Wat infiltrated the house and went after the children. Connor was then able to seize and detain her." Sophie had not figured out a way to keep the fact that Connor was already in the United States out of the conversation. "He had a lead on Pim Wat and followed her to my house, hoping to intercept her before she made a move. She is alive and safely contained."

"That *is* good news." McDonald made a harrumphing noise. "When and where can I pick her up?"

. . .

"We have conditions." Sophie focused on the road; after passing around scenic Diamond Head on the small two-lane artery, she'd entered an area of heavier traffic. She signaled and changed lanes. "I need you to send an agent to intervene on the part of one of our men, investigator Pierre Raveaux. He, too, was pursuing a lead and followed it to Corfu Island in Greece. He found Pim Wat's hideout there. Unfortunately, she was already here in Hawaii, and had booby-trapped the house. When he and his team of two men broke in, the place exploded. The men were killed, and Raveaux is injured. He's being held in a hospital on Corfu as a terrorist."

"I remember Raveaux." Sophie could visualize the way McDonald liked to lean back in his chair while thinking. "We have a Greek asset who is also a lawyer. I will send him to track down your man and get him out."

"Excellent. Then I will order a plane to pick up Raveaux on Corfu," Sophie said. "I have another condition."

"Why am I not surprised?"

"I would like Connor's agreement with the crime task force finalized in writing. Once you fax it to me, I will give you a location where you can retrieve Pim Wat."

"Consider it done."

"That's all for now. Let me know when your contact has found Raveaux, freed him, and transported him to our aircraft. When that last bit of paperwork is completed, we'll have a deal."

Sophie ended the call without a goodbye. It was important to keep the upper hand with a man like McDonald.

A memory flashed into her mind: Sophie kneeling, waiting in the doorway of her ex-husband Assan Ang's apartment in Hong Kong. Her eyes were down, her hands demurely clasped behind her back. Subservient to an extreme, she'd waited for Assan to come home from work as he'd told her she must—every day the apartment spotless, dinner simmering on the stove.

And Sophie, waiting on her knees to find out if he'd beat her that night, rape her, or worst of all, leave her alone in the dark of the windowless, soundproof panic room hidden inside the apartment.

Sophie exhaled audibly, clenching and releasing her hands on the steering wheel.

She'd come a long way since those days; Assan Ang would never lock her up again. Now she was the one in charge as her vile mother waited, tied up in the dark—as Sophie had endured so many times in that early, terrifying marriage.

She focused on navigating the downtown traffic until she reached Queens Hospital in downtown Honolulu, where her father had been taken. Secret Service agent Kate Smith had texted her Frank's room number and floor.

After she took a ticket and parked, Sophie exited the dimly lit garage and took the hospital stairs two a time, discharging physical tension as she made her way to her father's room, seesawing between hope and terror at what she'd find there.

36

Sophie stopped at the nurse's station on the floor, hoping to prepare herself before she entered her dad's room. "I'm Frank Smithson's daughter. Can I get an update on how he's doing?"

The nurse asked for her identification first, which Sophie found reassuring. She then pulled up her father's record on her computer. "Ambassador Smithson is conscious. but he's lost a lot of blood. He refused a transfusion, waiting for you to get here." The woman looked up at Sophie. "You're the same blood type. Are you willing to give blood?"

"Of course. As soon as possible." Sophies voice trembled. "Was he . . . was he poisoned? Is he going to live?"

The woman looked puzzled and glanced back at her screen. "They did a toxicology screen, and it came back negative for substances. Though I certainly can't guarantee anything, he seems to be stable."

Sophie let out a breath of relief. "Where do I go to donate blood? I'll visit him as soon as that is done."

She filled out forms and signed her consent, then went down a few floors to the hospital's lab. Resting comfortably on a padded chair, she watched a couple of pints fill plastic bags.

"Do you need any more?" Sophie asked when the nurse came to disconnect the apparatus.

The woman smiled. "You've given more than recommended in one session. You're going to be a little lightheaded and weak; take it easy. Drink this water and eat these orange slices before you go."

Sophie did so mechanically and left the lab as soon as they allowed her to.

She did indeed feel dizzy. This time she took the elevator to her father's floor and went straight to his room.

Frank was resting, propped on pillows with his eyes closed.

His color was gray and ashy; his dark lips were an unhealthy bluish color, though the monitors around him beeped and blipped in a peaceful pattern.

Sophie took the plastic chair beside his bed and picked up his large, well-shaped hand. His fingers were cold; she massaged them gently and lifted his palm to press it against her cheek.

"Don't cry, Sophie." His voice was a hoarse rasp. "I'm going to be okay. Pim Wat didn't get me. No poison on her blade, this time."

Sophie hadn't realized she was crying; she brushed the wetness off his hand. "I donated blood for your transfusion. We'll talk about you getting better after that."

Soon the doctor came in and discussed the transfusion with Frank. He signed the consent forms, then they hooked up a single bag of Sophie's platelets to his IV.

Sophie continued to hold Frank's hand as he drifted in and out of sleep; she woke herself with an abrupt twitch as a nurse leaned across her to adjust his IV. "All done. You should be feeling better soon, Ambassador."

"Thanks to my daughter, here." Frank caressed Sophie's scarred cheek with his thumb. "She's been the light of my life ever since she was born."

Sophie smiled. "Anything to help you feel better, Dad. Does the doctor know about your cancer? Will the transfusion make a difference with that?"

"Way above my pay grade." Frank's smile was wan. "But who

knows—I might be cured with my superhero daughter's blood running through my veins."

Sophie squeezed his hand. "I have news, Dad." When he'd given her his full attention, she went on. "Pim Wat is still alive. The woman you shot was an assassin, likely someone working for Mendoza or hired directly by my mother."

The color which had been returning to Frank's face drained abruptly away. His heart monitor began beeping a rapid, uneven tattoo. Sophie squeezed his limp fingers hard. "Rest easy, Dad. I thought you would be relieved to know."

"I wanted her dead," he ground out. "No longer a threat."

"She is neutralized. The CIA will be coming to get her shortly. She won't be our problem anymore." Sophie kissed Frank's big knuckles. "This is a good thing, Dad."

"Okay then, if you say so." The heart monitor began to even out. "It's true that I didn't want to kill her. She is your mother, after all, and I loved her once."

"Exactly. I knew that, *Pa*." Sophie used the Thai honorific. "You did what you had to do."

"And I'm still alive because the woman I killed wasn't her, and didn't use poison," Frank said. He pulled his hand away from hers and stroked his bedclothes restlessly. "Your mother is evil, Sophie."

"I know."

"What does it say about me, that I loved an evil woman? That I allowed her to use me, to extract secrets from me, for years?" The monitor began beeping again.

"Dad, it's okay. Take some deep breaths. It's all in the past." Sophie modeled breathing gently in through the nose, out through the mouth; he followed her example. Gradually they both calmed.

When the ambassador's vitals had stabilized, Sophie spoke again. "I don't think Pim Wat was always evil. She *was* always different; maybe she didn't react to things the way other people did, and her depression was real. She changed over time, as we all do, got worse if you will. And she's exceedingly good at what she does. She deceived not only you, but everyone around her. Yes, it hurts to have been a fool, to have been betrayed at such a deep level . . . but in the end, we prevailed." Sophie held Frank's gaze, staring into eyes that were darker brown and more deep-set than hers, but the same shape. "Now that Pim Wat's been caught, we can move on with our lives. Begin living again. With any luck at all, she won't ever make it out of Guantánamo Bay. McDonald is eager to—do what he does."

Frank shut his eyes and gave a brief nod. He took and squeezed Sophie's hand. Moments later he was asleep, his breathing evened out and deepened, his body gone slack.

"How is he doing?" A whisper from the door. Kate Smith, the very tall, blue-eyed brunette who had overseen Frank's Secret Service security detail for years, addressed Sophie.

Sophie stood up, gesturing for Kate to come in. "He's resting peacefully. He's expected to recover, and he just had a transfusion."

Kate entered the room and gave Sophie a hug. "I'm so glad! But you look wiped out. Why don't you go home and get some rest? I'll sit with him."

Katie would look after her father as well as Sophie could have; she could head home to her children and look in on Connor too. Sophie briefed the other woman on recent events and then took her leave, as Kate sat in the seat Sophie had vacated and picked up Frank's hand.

Gratitude swelled in Sophie's heart; she wasn't going to lose any of the men she loved today.

37

Day 10

Lei leaned forward in the seat of her flight to Maui, gripping the armrests as she gazed out the window. Swooping in a large turn to head into the wind as it landed, her Hawaiian Airlines plane bumped and bounced in the usual strong headwind of the Valley Isle.

Used to those conditions by now, Lei ignored the stressed-out reactions of the other passengers. She enjoyed the sight of the turquoise sea trimmed in white foam, the towering, sculpted curves of the Pali headlands and Haleakala, and the patchwork of fields that covered the waist of the figure eight shape of the island's central area.

Sophie's face flashed into Lei's mind—the toll of the last few days had been evident in the circles under her friend's eyes and the dull tone of her skin—but still, Sophie was a fighter. She'd handled the shooting and crisis outside her gate that had culminated in an intruder attack on Armita with remarkable poise and clear leadership. "You've come a long way, baby," Lei muttered. "All those men hop to it when you tell them to, including Connor."

Seeing her friend with Connor and witnessing the strong bond between them had washed away the last of Lei's concerns about the mysterious cyber vigilante tech genius Sophie had chosen. The man clearly adored Sophie, enough to give up his powerful position as the Master of the Yām Khûmkạn in Thailand—and his vigilante activities, too.

If he was pardoned, all would be well.

After Jake's death, and all she'd been through with her awful mother, Sophie deserved a little happiness.

"Make that a lot of happiness," Lei muttered. She was glad they'd been able to clear up the issues that had created a barrier between them, but Lei wouldn't be surprised if secrets were an ongoing theme in her relationship with Sophie; strange people and events surrounded her friend.

Once the plane made its turn, it dropped rapidly and soon came to a bumpy stop on the tarmac. Lei glanced at the familiar gyration of the coconut palms around the airport with a smile and activated her phone, looking for a text from Abe Torufu.

Sure enough, her partner had sent her a note that he'd pick her up; they had an hour or so to get into position for the takedown of the egg sellers.

Lei's pulse picked up. "Perfect. Just time to grab something to eat." Her stomach rumbled loudly; she'd grabbed a granola bar from Armita on the way out of Sophie's house but hadn't had anything to eat since she and Jones grabbed burgers on the way there.

She texted Torufu about getting food. The big man was agreeable. Soon she was tossing her carry-on into the back of his truck. "Ichiban?" Lei asked, sliding into the passenger seat beside him.

"Sure. I want to get into position a bit before the time of the meet, though," Torufu said. "I've already talked to airport security about access and backup support. The buy is going down at the interisland cargo area of the airport. Makes sense; it's a lot quieter, with fewer people and security around. The eggs will be packaged for transport and will need to be passed off to the buyer from off-island."

Ichiban, Lei's favorite little hole-in-the-wall restaurant, was only a few minutes away. The staff knew them, so in mere moments Lei was scooping savory saimin noodles into her mouth as Torufu did the same across the table from her.

"How's Sophie doing?" Torufu asked.

"Lotta drama going on in her personal life." Lei filled Torufu in with a thumbnail sketch of the events of the day.

"Holy . . . no wonder you were eager to get home!" The Tongan's eyes went comically round. "Glad you're back in one piece!"

"Me too." Lei set her empty bowl aside and waved for the check. "Let's get over to the airport and take down some egg-nappers."

Torufu showed Lei the student photos of the two Paradise Preparatory Academy boys that had stolen eggs from the sanctuary. "The buyer is from overseas. My guess is, the boys will collect their payment, then hand over the eggs. But I don't know where they're meeting, exactly."

With the help of the airport personnel, the two detectives positioned themselves near the check-in area for cargo.

Lei pretended to be a bored local girl, kicking a slipper-clad foot, as she waited with a large, string-wrapped fake package on her lap.

Torufu got behind the weighing counter and, beside one of the service people, pretended to be a loader, hefting boxes onto a trolley.

Lei scanned the comings and goings of customers and staff, watching for a pair of teen boys.

When the perps showed up, it was suddenly: one moment the entry area was empty, the next two teens in low-slung pants, carrying between them a large red-and-white plastic cooler with a bungee cord around it, approached from the parking lot.

Both wore sunglasses and pulled-down ball caps, so their faces were hard to make out—but Lei felt sure these were the kids whose pictures she'd seen.

The pair approached Torufu at the cargo check-in counter. "Can you hold this back here for us?" the taller boy asked Torufu. He extended a hand holding a bill folded between his fingers. "Just for a few minutes. We're trying to decide if we're going to ship this or not."

Torufu gave a toothy smile and waved away the bribe. "No problem." He took the cooler carefully and set it behind the counter, exchanging a humorous glance with Lei. "I'll take good care of it."

The boys turned and walked toward the open bay leading to the tarmac.

Approaching from the aircraft area was a short, older Asian man wearing a fishing hat pulled down over sunglasses and a loud aloha shirt covered in parrots. "You boys know where I can see some unique sights?" he asked.

"Sure," the bigger kid said. "I've got a few ideas." The pair led the parrot-covered man over to the shadows, talking intently.

Lei frowned, glancing at Torufu. When should they make a move? So far, nothing incriminating had happened, and truth was, she couldn't make a positive ID on the kids without being able to see their faces more clearly.

But then something hidden in a folded newspaper changed hands. The three of them turned and headed back to the shipping desk. "We'll take our cooler now," Tall Boy said.

"Nope." Torufu lifted his badge and held it up. "Maui Police Department. You're all under arrest."

Both boys froze, then ran for the entrance. The buyer spun and ran for the runway area.

"You get the kids, you're faster!" Torufu yelled, exploding out from behind the counter to chase the man in the parrot shirt.

Lei was already on her feet and moving, having tossed the hat and box the minute the boys bolted. She bellowed in her best cop voice: "Stop! Police!"

But the teens didn't stop, and at the entrance they split and headed in opposite directions.

Lei chose the taller boy who'd done the talking. She poured on speed, glad she still ran on a regular basis and always wore her athletic shoes.

The kid hadn't done that. Hampered by ill-fitting, loose pants and a pair of lug sole boots that must have been fashionable somewhere, the boy was slower than he should have been. He tried to lose her by dodging in and out of traffic as he headed for the parking lot. Lei overtook him on the sidewalk and shoved him between the shoulder blades with enough force to send him sprawling.

Once he was down, she landed on his back with a knee and pulled his arms up, cuffing him and reciting the Miranda warning as she did so.

When the boy got his breath back, she helped him up and shepherded him back to the shipping area, where she met Torufu on the sidewalk with his prize, the buyer in the aloha shirt—and handcuffs.

Torufu called Dr. Powers from the Maui Albatross Sanctuary after checking that the eggs, carefully wrapped inside the cooler with a battery-powered heat source near them, were unharmed.

They took the perps back through the cargo area, enjoying a bit of applause from the employees, and put the two in the back of a cruiser to ride downtown for booking. They sent a uniform to look for the other boy at his house, then got back into the truck and headed to the Maui Albatross Sanctuary to meet the biologist and return the eggs to their parent birds.

Torufu glanced over at Lei as they neared the windswept wild area of the sanctuary, only half an hour from downtown Kahului. Their eyes met; his were sparkling, and Lei answered with a dimple. "Good day?"

"The best day."

That little exchange was left over from when they'd worked bomb squad together; every day they hadn't had an explosive was the best day.

Dr. Powers met them in the familiar dirt parking lot. She was accompanied by Mahmoud Gadish; the two got out of the biologist's truck. Lei hid surprise that the widower had the wherewithal to come so quickly after losing his wife.

Lei approached the pair, Torufu at her back carrying the red cooler.

"I'm so deeply sorry for your loss." Though not a hugger, she opened her arms on impulse. Gadish stepped into them, releasing a deep, shuddering sigh as he embraced her. "Your wife should have been here with us to return these precious eggs."

Gadish stepped back, and she saw a glimmer of the fanatical light Sari had shown in talking about the albatrosses. "She could be with us, even now, in one of those eggs."

Lei dropped her gaze, unable to come up with a response.

Torufu stepped up to grip the man's shoulder. "I'm sorry for your loss. Glad you could join us this morning."

"The birds are in mourning, but they haven't left their nests," Dr. Powers said. The biologist wore a safari hat and was slung about with gear. "Follow me and we will drop an egg off at each one of the nests." She patted her camera case. "To document the reunion."

"Are you sure the eggs are still good?" Lei frowned, pointing to the cooler. "Shouldn't we verify they're live, or something?"

Dr. Powers opened the lid of the cooler and checked the temperature with a hand. "Looks like those kids did their homework. If the eggs were kept at an even temperature within the range they can survive, they should be okay. If not, they will fail to hatch—and that is a more normal process than having an egg stolen for the parent birds. You'll see what I mean when we reach the nesting area."

Lei and Torufu followed the two sanctuary board members down the now-familiar trail into the reservation area, and through the gate. This time, they turned left and took a different path than the one that had led to the crashed drone.

Lei pointed to the security cameras atop the fence. "Those working all right?"

"They sure are. Could use help monitoring them, though—we've had to fix a couple already. They're pretty weather-sensitive," the biologist said over her shoulder.

Around a large boulder, sheltered from the wind beneath a bush, stood a couple of albatrosses. The mated pair were close together, their heads resting on each other's breasts. They seemed to be leaning on each other.

Lei covered her mouth with her hand—their pose was so touching. The emotion in it mirrored the grief and love she and Stevens had shared when she lost their baby at four months into the pregnancy. She blinked away tears, watching as Torufu set down the cooler.

The doc, sliding her hands into leather mitts, reached into the container, and picked up one of the carefully wrapped eggs. "I'm wearing gloves, so my scent and skin oils won't contaminate the shell," she explained, removing the toweling the boys had wrapped around the egg. "It looks like they took care with these."

"Protecting their investment, the little jerks," Torufu growled.

"Quiet now," the doc hushed. She crouched low, holding the egg, which was about the size of a mango, on her open palm.

The birds, large enough to do damage if they chose to with their heavy wings and long, razor-sharp bills, separated and watched closely but without fear as Dr. Powers approached and set the egg gently into the empty nest.

"Now, if only they accept it," Gadish said.

"If only," Lei echoed.

The biologist backed away, gesturing for the group to get behind the boulder, out of sight.

Lei, Torufu, Gadish and Dr. Powers hunkered down, but peeked around the boulder to watch as the birds investigated the egg. They walked over to the nest, clacking their beaks in agitation, for all the world as if speaking to each other—and then, after reaching in to adjust the egg's position, one of them stepped into the nest and gently lowered itself to sit with the egg tucked between its feet, cushioned by the thick feathers of its breast.

The other bird, still chattering, preened, and then settled carefully beside its mate, smoothing dazzling white feathers over the poofy spot where the egg nestled with its beak.

Tears welled in Lei's eyes. "That's just so damn beautiful."

Everyone agreed.

The group repeated the process two more times and were able to see the parent albatrosses accept the eggs.

When Lei and Torufu got back into his truck with the empty cooler, they exchanged a smile once more.

"Good day?" Lei said.

"The best day ever," Torufu said, and turned on the truck.

38

Day 11

Sophie stood on the blue ceramic tiles of the entry of her house midday of the next day, waiting for the CIA to arrive.

Dressed in a pair of easy movement black pants, a white button-down blouse with cap sleeves that showed off her toned arms, her favorite Tahitian pearls at her ears, Sophie was ready for anything—even dealing with Agent McDonald, his minions, and her mother.

She'd called in a favor from a doctor she knew through her Security Solutions position, and the woman had come to the house and examined Connor. She'd set his leg and equipped him with a light-weight modern cast and a crutch.

"You're doing remarkably well, considering," the doctor had said, brushing glass off Connor's skin. "These lacerations are barely showing. Other than the broken leg, which is going to set cleanly—you're in surprisingly good shape."

Sophie and Connor had exchanged a look; he must have been working to accelerate his healing. The glass that peppered his bedsheets had been ejected by his skin as it closed. Sophie wasn't going to say anything about that, and neither was Connor.

After the doctor left, she'd given Connor a sponge bath, which they'd both enjoyed. Armita and Feirn had cooked dinner; they'd eaten with the family in the dining room. Sophie and Armita put the children to bed, and she and Connor had spent another platonic night together.

Sophie's mouth softened in a smile, remembering the sweet hours as they'd slept in each other's arms.

She'd barely thought about Pim Wat at all—hadn't been down to the basement to check on her mother. Sophie'd left her there, just as she'd said she would.

McDonald had contacted her early in the morning to let her know that the CIA lawyer, working with police, had been able to clear Raveaux of anything but breaking and entering Pim Wat's place. He'd arrived in Honolulu the previous evening on the plane she'd sent for him and was presumably home resting. She'd call him soon and hear all about his adventure in Greece.

Sophie smoothed her hair, which she'd pulled back into a sleek updo, as the gate alarm chimed. McDonald would arrive any moment with Connor's immunity agreement and a private transport to take Pim Wat away, permanently. She'd sent Armita and Feirn to the nursery with the children for the duration, and Connor was resting in the guest room, out of view of the CIA man and his team.

The gate retracted.

Sophie's security detail approached the large black government SUV that drove in. Clement and Bill checked it over and verified IDs, allowing the CIA men to keep their weapons.

At last, McDonald hefted his bulk out of the vehicle. He ambled over to Sophie. "Looking great as usual, Ms. Smithson." McDonald's voice was hearty. His glittery little eyes gleamed; the man couldn't wait to get his hands on Pim Wat.

"And you seem healthy as well, Agent McDonald." Sophie suppressed a shiver at what her mother would face, but Pim Wat had earned what she had coming.

"These men are with me to assist in transporting the prisoner should she get physical."

One of two agents trailing McDonald held up an old-fashioned canvas straitjacket with a grin. "For her safety. No throwing herself down a set of stairs while in our custody."

A flash of memory—Pim Wat had done just that, trying to kill herself before she could be turned over to the CIA the last time Sophie had apprehended her.

The tickle of discomfort that danced down her spine was harder to ignore this time.

Did she really care what happened to Pim Wat?

No, she did not.

The woman deserved every torture they came up with for her.

Sophie firmed her jaw. "Come in, please." She turned and led the agents inside. "Show me Connor's agreement and proof of Raveaux's release."

McDonald gave his jowly chuckle. "Aren't you a hard-ass." He reached into the pocket of a loose pair of Bermuda shorts. "Here you go. And a picture on my phone of Raveaux."

Sophie took McDonald's phone first, gazing down at Pierre's face. His skin was pockmarked with cuts, both of his eyes were puffy and dark with bruising, and his expression was bleak; but he was standing upright with a crutch at the top of a set of stairs, ready to enter the Security Solutions jet.

Sophie took the papers and handed the phone back to McDonald. "Text the photo to me." She walked over to the kitchen counter, where a colored glass spot lamp provided a handy pool of light. She illuminated the agreement and read it rapidly, noting the signatures of the law enforcement agencies at the bottom and the date. She held up her phone and took a picture, then folded the paper and slid it into her pocket, turning back to McDonald. "Now I'll show you where we've been holding Pim Wat. But I won't be accompanying you. You will have to deal with her yourselves."

"Not a problem." McDonald gave a wolffish grin.

Sophie checked on Armita and the children in the nursery, and then went to join Connor with Feirn in the guest room while the CIA men were in the basement.

He'd moved his casted leg to the side of the bed and sat up. "I heard voices. What's going on?"

She handed the agreement to him. "McDonald is here getting Pim Wat."

"I want to see her." He glanced up from the paper, sea-blue eyes intense.

Sophie frowned and shook her head. "Nothing good can come of it."

"Get me my crutch. Something to use to walk."

Feirn brought the crutch and helped Connor out of the room and down the hall to the kitchen. Sophie and Connor were standing at the kitchen's island when McDonald emerged, alone, from the panic room's dumbwaiter. "Your elevator sure is cramped."

"It's designed for two adults of normal size," Sophie said. "You are not of normal size."

"No shit, Sherlock." McDonald's face was greasy with sweat, and four distinct nail marks were etched down one cheek. He fished a handkerchief out of his pocket and held it to his bleeding face. "We have her in hand, though it took a bit of effort. She'll be up with one of my men next."

Sophie bit her tongue to keep from asking any more questions. Pim Wat was no longer her problem.

A few minutes later, the elevator opened again, disgorging a small, struggling figure hidden under one of the blue emergency blankets Sophie had stowed in the basement. One of the agents gripped her by the arm, and he wasn't gentle as he shoved Pim Wat out of the pantry.

She stumbled and landed in a heap like a bundle of laundry.

"Why is she covered? Did you beat her already?" Sophie stepped forward and yanked the blanket off Pim Wat.

Her mother wore the canvas straitjacket the agent had shown Sophie. With her arms so tightly bound, she'd hit the tile floor when she fell; a red contusion was forming on her forehead. Her strange green eyes were completely demented, bloodshot and bouncing around the room without recognition. The soiled gag Armita had put on her was gone. She smelled strongly of urine.

But she hadn't been beaten.

The elevator disgorged the final agent, looking somewhat worse for wear. "You have a bit of a mess to clean up down there."

Sophie ignored him. She squatted down to Pim Wat's level. "Mother. I want you to know things didn't have to end this way."

Pim Wat stared at Sophie without recognition.

She glanced past Sophie and growled—she had spotted Connor.

Before any of them could grab her, Pim Wat leaped from her knees to her feet and launched herself at Connor. She barreled into him, hitting him in the midsection with her head. Momentum bore the two of them to the ground. Fierce as a trapped feral animal and just as terrifying, Pim Wat kicked and bit at him.

Connor rolled away to his feet with no apparent loss of mobility due to the cast. He caught Pim Wat by the strap on the back of the straitjacket, lifting her with one hand. She kicked and writhed, spitting and growling. "May you rot in the hell of your own making, Pim Wat."

He handed the writhing woman to the two agents. They each took a side and dragged her to the front door of the house, down the verandah, and all the way out to the waiting SUV, where they tossed her into the back.

Sophie handed Connor his makeshift crutch as he faced McDonald.

"And now you know why we put a blanket over her head," the CIA man said. "Looks like she drew blood." He flicked a finger at Connor's bleeding ear. "No shame. She got me too. Real wildcat, that one."

Connor's face reflected nothing but detached regret. "Please don't let her escape again."

McDonald scowled. "She won't get away this time. She no longer has the Master of the Yām Khûmkạn on her side."

"That's certainly true." Connor inclined his head. "Until we meet again, then."

"Yep. I'll be in touch." McDonald gave a terse nod and followed his men out.

Sophie's heart was still pounding from Pim Wat's surprise attack on Connor. She embraced him; his heart was thundering, too, though he'd given no sign of distress. "Are you okay?"

"I will be. You?" He pulled back a bit to search her eyes.

"Now that she's gone, yes." Sophie wrapped her arms tightly around his neck and pressed close.

He dropped the crutch and squeezed her length against his, his hands dropping to her waist, smoothing her back. "It's over. She's gone."

"Amen to that."

Sophie rested her head on his shoulder and sighed deeply, closing her eyes, sinking into his hug. Connor was several perfect inches taller, and her head fit nicely beneath his cheek. They leaned into each other, each drawing strength from the other; she hoped it would always be that way.

39

Day 11

Raveaux had slept in the stateroom for most of the flight home on the Security Solutions jet Sophie had sent to Corfu to pick him up. The authorities on Corfu had let Raveaux go after the arrival of the lawyer the CIA had sent. He had thrown his weight around and translated Raveaux's statement accurately.

Broken ribs and internal bruising continued to cause a good deal of pain, so Pierre was a bit loopy from medications when he staggered out of the bed to take his seat before the plane landed in Honolulu. He scrubbed his face with a hand and thought of shaving —but Sophie wouldn't expect him to be looking his best; she'd understand.

The thought of seeing her at the gate energized his battered body and cleared his foggy brain. He gazed out the window as the jet lowered through dazzling cumulus clouds toward the airstrip, whose runway began just beyond the brilliant azure and turquoise water of Pearl Harbor.

The bodies of Sam and Rab, too burnt to identify, had been cremated.

He'd claimed them as colleagues, identified them for the medical examiner as "his men," mercenaries from Thailand who came with him as a private investigator to gather information on a dangerous assassin hiding on their peaceful Greek island.

With the lawyer backing him, they'd believed him; the evidence of a rigged house had validated him further.

Raveaux had been given a small packet of ashes to remember them by. He couldn't remember their full names in Thai, nor spell them, so "Sam "and "Rab" were written on the clear plastic Ziploc bags which the lawyer had stowed in a small earthenware pot with a lid.

"A sad souvenir from Corfu," he'd said, handing the lidded jar to Raveaux as he got on the plane.

Raveaux reached into his leather satchel and took out the makeshift urn, about the size of an apple. Made of plain red, bisque-fired clay, the jar wasn't even decorated.

"What a keepsake," Raveaux muttered. His eyes stung; he slid the jar back into the satchel and refocused on the view.

He'd see Sophie soon; he'd feel better then.

The plane circled, dropping down to parallel the dramatic green corrugated peaks of the Koʻolau Mountains. Moments later, the jet touched down and taxied over to the private aircraft entrance gate.

Raveaux only had his carry-on; he thanked the pilot and copilot as he exited, one arm tucked tight against his side to stabilize his ribs. Walking across the hot black asphalt to the entry gate took a long, painful time.

The plane had stopped to refuel in Seattle, where he had gone through customs, so that ordeal didn't have to be done again. As Raveaux passed through the entry turnstile, he scanned for Sophie's tall, slender height.

Instead, he spotted a tiny woman wearing a bright orange hat and a big smile: Hermione Leede.

Contrasting with the hat, Leede wore a turquoise skirt suit the color of a parakeet's plumage. She moved through the crowd toward him. "Pierre! You look in much better health than I was led to believe!"

His gaze flickered past Heri to search the crowd. "Glad to be able to walk," he said.

"Sophie's not coming. She sent me to pick you up and take you home." Heri fiddled with her sparkly glasses. "You're disappointed."

Raveaux rallied with an effort. "Just surprised. Sophie got me out of a locked Greek hospital, where I was under arrest on a serious charge. No small feat. Thought we'd update about the case." He stepped forward to give Heri a careful hug, knocking her hat askew. "Thanks so much for coming to get me. I know how busy you are."

"And don't you forget it. My time is quite valuable." Heri adjusted the hat to its former jaunty angle. "I have news. Much news. But I'll wait until we're in the car to give it to you. Listening ears, you know."

Raveaux tugged at one of his lobes. "Lucky to be able to hear you at all. I lost an eardrum and this side's damaged, so if I seem to ignore you . . . I just didn't catch something."

"Oh, no! What else got hurt?" Heri took his good arm, as was her habit; he liked the feeling of her petite warm presence at his side.

"Bruised organs and broken ribs. A concussion. The hearing issues. All things that will mend with time, though the headache I've had—*mon Dieu!*"

"It's amazing you can walk at all!" She squeezed Raveaux's arm fervently. "Right over here. I parked in the handicapped stall, naughty me, since I knew you wouldn't be in shape for a long trek."

Raveaux belted in and braced himself as Heri hopped into the driver's seat of the massive Cadillac she drove with pedal extenders and a pillow under her bottom to see over the dash.

"Tell me the big news."

"Give me a moment." Heri grasped the wheel in ring-covered, glittering hands. "Getting out of this airport is always tricky." She tore the hat off and tossed it in the back seat. "Can't have anything getting in the way of visibility."

"Indeed." Raveaux gripped the sissy strap as Heri backed up and spun the Cadillac around with enough g-forces to throw him back against the headrest. "Ow!"

"Oh, my goodness. Your head injury!" She put on the brakes, and he bounced off the dash. "Sorry! I'll be more careful."

"Please. Have mercy." Raveaux grabbed whatever he could to stabilize himself as she switched lanes with no apparent signal or safety check.

Once they were on the freeway, she patted his arm. "Relax, Pierre. Have I ever been in an accident?"

"I don't know. Have you?" He was in too much pain to be amused.

"No, I have not. But quite a pileup happened in front of Sophie's fancy new compound the other day." Heri launched into an outrageous story of a full-frontal attack by a Pim Wat look-alike on Connor using a rental car. Heri described Connor as "Sophie's boyfriend," and seemed to relish the denouement in which Sophie's father shot the woman and ended up in the hospital. In a final twist, a dramatic attack on Armita in the house revealed the real Pim Wat. "And that should bring you up to speed on what's been happening on this side of the world."

"I see why Sophie didn't have time to come meet me at the airport."

"Nor did she have inclination to do so," Heri said crisply. "Give it up, Pierre; she's just not into you, as they say in America."

Raveaux fingered the shape of the jar in his satchel without replying.

Heri cranked a left turn into his building's parking lot and stopped in front of his apartment by hitting the curb; Raveaux gritted his teeth.

Raveaux gathered what shreds of dignity he could scratch together and reached for the door handle. "Thanks for the ride, Heri." He opened the door and used the handle to pull his aching body upright. "In future, I'll do the driving whenever we go anywhere."

Heri's grin was impudent. "As long as we go somewhere."

Raveaux almost smiled. "I'll call you when I'm back on my feet." He shut the door and headed for his apartment's walkway.

He could feel Heri's gaze on his back, almost hear her berating herself for being too blunt, wondering if he would have invited her inside if he hadn't been hurting, if she hadn't stung him further with her words about Sophie. He knew Heri well enough by now to know all that, and to like her for it; even so, he couldn't find the energy to turn back and give her a reassuring wave.

Raveaux fumbled with his keys and got the front door open, the kettledrum of his brain pounding. He couldn't wait to get to the bathroom and down a big glass of water with a handful of painkillers, then fall into bed. He was exhausted and hurt all over, not least his heart.

Lisette sat on the shiny clean tile in front of the door as he opened it. She looked fat and glossy; the boy had cared for her well. Even so, she mewed her displeasure at his absence.

He set down the satchel and scooped the lanky kitten up as he headed for the bathroom. "It's good to be home, *ma petite*. And to be missed by someone I don't have to say another word to."

He kissed her head, and she purred in reply.

Day 12

Night surrounded Connor and Sophie as they sat on the bench under the *hala* tree. The waves, their power banked by a barrier reef a hundred yards out, purled and splashed gently on the beach on the other side of the transparent wall Sophie was so proud of. The two baby coconut palms she'd planted swayed and danced, framing a view she clearly treasured.

Rightly so. They could sit here and watch the moon on the ocean, safe and secure, sheltered even from the breeze that snagged the surface of the water, fragmenting it into a kaleidoscope of subtle colors. Inside the house, sleeping and safe, were precious children, Armita, and Feirn. Watching over the family were their dogs and a trained, caring security team.

Sophie had done this; she'd created this protected place, away from the rest of the world, where they could relax, recharge—and hopefully, reconnect.

Connor sneaked a glance at Sophie's profile.

Moonlight painted her tawny skin with a pale glow that highlighted her forehead, the slope of her nose, the rich curves of her lips and cheeks. How he loved her.

Just to be here, at her home, with the threats they'd faced behind them—the sense of freedom, of hope and possibility, almost made him dizzy.

And yet, he couldn't forget all who'd died so that this moment could happen. Their faces surrounded him: Jake, Nine, Sam and Rab, and so many more. Even the former Master was present, watching with a benevolent purple gaze.

"What?" Sophie turned to him, smiling. "You're staring at me. Do I have something on my nose?"

"I can't quite believe this is real." He could hardly speak past the lump in his throat.

Sophie had been physically remote since he moved into the house: a fleeting touch on his shoulder, a peck on the cheek, a hug, leaning against him or snuggling platonically had been the extent of their touch—but now, she cupped his jaw in her hand and kissed him.

Oh, that kiss.

He slowed his breath, his heartbeat, the very movement of the blood in his veins so he could more deeply inhabit the moment when she lowered her guard and took him all the way in.

Humility and gratitude were the flavors on his tongue as he tasted her; tears flowed freely and added salt.

She pulled back and stoked his cheek, his jaw, the muscle of his shoulder. "Why are you sad?"

"I'm not sad. I'm just . . ." Words failed him. He ducked his head to rest it on her breast. She pulled him close, stroking his hair, his shoulders, his back. His body stirred in response.

"They're always here with us, aren't they? Even my mother," she murmured.

"Yes."

"Let's go to my room and leave them outside." She stood, and took his hand, and helped him with his crutch. They went up the steps of the verandah into the house and closed the door behind them.

Want to stay in this world? Grab HIDDEN FALLS, Paradise Crime Mysteries #16 with Lei, next! Or, if you haven't started that series, begin with BLOOD ORCHIDS, free. You can also get TWO FREE full length Toby Neal novels by signing up for my newsletter, HERE.

Thanks so much for joining Sophie and Lei on this adventure. If you enjoyed the story, please leave a review! They matter more than you know.

As with all my stories, this book began with an idea based on a real-life Hawaii issue.

My love and respect for the *moli* began in my early twenties. My parents built a house in Princeville on Kauai, and when I visited them, we made a family habit of taking an evening walk to say hello to the majestic albatrosses who nested on one of the bluffs near their home. This was no bird sanctuary; it was just a vacant lot on a bluff above the ocean, with the right wind and other conditions for their nesting and launching needs.

I was smitten with the birds' great beauty, huge size, gentle nature, and the passionate attachments to their mates and chicks that they demonstrated. We lived beside them in peace for years, and our biggest worries back then, were the stray cats and loose dogs known to prey upon the helpless chicks or eggs.

Fast forward to the year 2015, when my husband and I rented a beach house on the North Shore of Oahu and brought our adult children over to spend a wonderful beachfront holiday with us. Mike and I wanted them to experience the huge waves and invigorating surf scene at Pipeline (which inspired the book Rip Tides.) One day we took a hike out to Ka'ena Point, the same hike Sophie, Pierre, and Marcus Kamuela take in the book. We visited the albatrosses inside their fenced sanctuary there, and were amazed, as I'd been on Kauai, at their peaceful, fearless tolerance toward us.

Two days later, a real "Moli Massacre" occurred—several perpetrators broke into the sanctuary and killed most of the nesting albatrosses and their eggs and chicks, for no reason anyone could figure out.

I transformed my outraged grief that such a thing had occurred, by solving the crime on paper with a team of investigators I knew could take it on.

It has brought me a measure of comfort to learn that the decimated albatross population has come back a surprising degree, and even more people are looking out for the birds at Ka'ena than before.

That said, there is no albatross sanctuary on Maui in reality—Maui has too many feral cats, most likely, for the birds to find it an appealing spot to raise their vulnerable young, but I enjoyed pretending there was one.

As we wrap up this thriller, Pim Wat is still around, but safely contained for the moment. I, like you, breathed a sigh of relief that she's where she deserves to be for the indefinite future.

Until next time, I'll be writing!

Toby Neal

P.S. Don't forget to grab your FREE BOOKS by signing up for my newsletter, if you haven't already! Mahalo!

ABOUT THE AUTHOR

Kirkus Reviews calls Neal's writing, *"persistently riveting. Masterly."*

Award-winning, USA Today bestselling social worker turned author Toby Neal grew up on the island of Kaua`i in Hawaii. Neal is a mental health therapist, a career that has informed the depth and complexity of the characters in her stories. Neal's mysteries and thrillers explore the crimes and issues of Hawaii from the bottom of the ocean to the top of volcanoes. Fans call her stories, *"Immersive, addicting, and the next best thing to being there."*

Neal also pens romance and romantic thrillers as Toby Jane and writes memoir/nonfiction under TW Neal.

Visit tobyneal.net for more ways to stay in touch!
or
Join my Facebook readers group, *Friends Who Like Toby Neal Books*, for special giveaways and perks.

Made in the USA
Las Vegas, NV
07 July 2022